Always You

(A Murphy Brothers Story)

The Potter's House Books (Two)

BY
JENNIFER RODEWALD

Always You

Copyright © 2020 Jennifer Rodewald.

All rights reserved. No part of this publication may be reproduced, distributed, or transmitted in any form or by any means, including photocopying, recording, or other electronic or mechanical methods, without the prior written permission of the publisher, except in the case of brief quotations embodied in critical reviews and certain other noncommercial uses permitted by copyright law. For permission requests, write to the publisher, addressed "Attention: Permissions Coordinator," at the address below.

ISBN: 978-1-7347421-0-7

Any references to events, real people, or real places are used fictitiously. Names, characters, and places are products of the author's imagination, and any similarities to real events are purely accidental.

Front cover image Lightstock.com. Design by Jennifer Rodewald.

First printing edition 2020.

Rooted Publishing

McCook, NE 69001

Email: jen@authorjenrodewald.com

https://authorjenrodewald.com/

All Scripture quotations, unless otherwise indicated, are taken from the Holy Bible, New International Version®, NIV®. Copyright ©1973, 1978, 1984, 2011 by Biblica, Inc. Used by permission of Zondervan. All rights reserved worldwide. www.zondervan.com The "NIV" and "New International Version" are trademarks registered in the United States Patent and Trademark Office by Biblica, Inc.

The twenty-four books that form The Potter's House Books Series (Two) are linked by the theme of hope, redemption, and second chances. They are all stand-alone books and can be read in any order. Books will become progressively available from January 7, 2020.

Book 1: *The Hope We Share*, by Juliette Duncan
Book 2: *Beyond the Deep*, by Kristen M. Fraser
Book 3: *Honor's Reward*, by Mary Manners
Book 4: *Hands of Grace*, by Brenda S. Anderson
Book 5: *Always You*, by Jen Rodewald
Book 6: *Her Cowboy Forever*, by Dora Hiers
Book 7: *Changed Somehow*, by Chloe Flanagan
Books 8: *Sweet Scent of Forgiveness*, by Delia Latham
Books 9–24 to be announced

Copyright © 2020 Jennifer Rodewald
All rights reserved.

*Teach me your way, LORD, that I may rely on your faithfulness;
give me an undivided heart, that I may fear your name.
Psalm 86:11*

Jennifer Rodewald

Chapter One
(in which Lauren meets a man at the airport)

She was gonna throw up.

Lauren squeezed her eyes tight, trying desperately to focus on the audible version of a story the talented Tamara Leigh had penned. But alas, even the commanding distraction of the Wulfriths would not take her mind away from the facts.

She was going to puke.

Somebody please just let me off this plane. I'm really going to throw up!

Another arctic gale rocked the cabin as the aircraft sat like a lame duck on the tarmac. The strong winter storm had snuck onto the Pacific West Coast like Santa Claus on Christmas Eve, only this visitor was not leaving any gifts of kindness.

Served her right, she guessed, leaving her home, her family, and all the expectations she was certain she could never meet. If she worked harder to conform, tried to be a bit more like Ashley, maybe then...

Who was she kidding? Lauren knew full well she was not politician material. Economics confused her. Politics, frankly, made her angry, and she made an effort to avoid them as much as she could. Hard to do when your father was a senator. Her studies in history, while intriguing, did not make her buzz with anticipation. And just like her mother, Lauren hated arguing. Hated it. So while her younger sister, Ashley, became the new shining star of the Matlock family, following closely in their father's astutely successful footsteps, Lauren found a job on the other side of the country, doing something entirely different than anyone in her family had ever done. Something that, she hoped and prayed, would never have anything to do with politics, ever.

As she thought about the rise of mountains that she'd seen in the pamphlet, the shimmering waters of Lake Tahoe that she had stared at for an inordinate amount of time on her computer screen, and the delicious idea of embarking on grand adventures in the middle of God's creation, her heart lightened—even with the swirl of encroaching sickness that refused to abate. The glory and splendor of all of it would be right at her fingertips. Just outside her door, her everyday life right in the midst of it, as she took on a new role at a small resort in North Lake Tahoe.

Her stomach lurched.

That was, if she survived the flight. At the moment it didn't seem likely. The wind battered against the fuselage, causing the cabin to shudder again. Lauren pushed Pause on the medieval tale she'd been trying to listen to and gripped the armrest at her side.

"You're okay, sweetie." The gentle voice came from her left, from Cindy, the older woman who shared the row and had kindly offered to sit next to the window when they'd discussed how Lauren didn't always handle air travel well.

Lauren wanted to say she'd be fine, but all that escaped her lips was a pathetic moan.

"Oh, honey, I'm so sorry." Cindy patted her back. "Surely they'll let us off this plane soon."

"Hope so." Lauren whimpered. Her head lolled as a wave of nausea had her rocking forward, jamming her elbows onto her knees and gripping the back of her head.

"Here's a bag here, sweetie."

A waxy paper sack was pushed into her palm

Awesome. It'd been a completely full flight from her connection in Denver, no seats available, and she was going to vomit right there in a bag while they were all trapped on a plane in the middle of a blizzard with no end in sight. This was the epitome of a nightmare. The evening could not get worse.

The overhead cabin dinged, alerting passengers of an important message, and the voice of her salvation came over the speakers. "Ladies and gentlemen, I'm sorry for the delay. We have clearance to go to an alternative gate. Sit tight a few more minutes, folks. We will be deplaning shortly."

As tears burned against her eyelids, Lauren breathed multiple pleas and thank-yous to heaven above. *Please let me off this plane. Please don't let me puke next to this nice lady. And thank You that we made it here safely.*

Now to get her feet on the ground. Maybe then the vertigo would stop. Maybe then she could go back to looking forward to the new life she was flying into—airsickness and all.

The plane lurched forward as they taxied toward the newly opened gate.

Just hold on, she thought repeatedly. *Hold on just a little longer.*

Clutching her carry-on and the wax-paper puke bag that she was supposed to use if she *couldn't* hold on, she stood when the captain announced their arrival and that they could leave the plane and thank you very much for flying with them. Lauren wobbled to her feet. The dizzying nausea claimed her again, and she shut her eyes against the world and the sensation and the fear that no, she was not going to make it. She was going to vomit right there in the middle of everyone.

Cindy squeezed Lauren's elbow. "It's okay, sweetie, if you need to throw up. You just go ahead and do it. I have kids. It's not as if I've never dealt with puke before."

Lauren tried to open her eyes and give the kind woman a weak smile. She was quite certain it came out like a squint and a grimace. Hardly mattered. She'd never see her again. She hoped so at least, for the sake of her quickly failing dignity. Finally the people in front of them began to move forward, and the woman at her side allowed Lauren to pass in front of her. Cindy's steady hand remained on her back while she guided her down the aisle, out the Jetway, and into the airport terminal.

Oh goodness. She was off the plane. She should be getting better now. Any moment. The nausea should stop. Her head should clear. Her stomach should stop rioting.

No. That was *not* going to happen.

Still clutching the drag handle to her carry-on, Lauren whipped a panicked gaze around, desperately searching for a restroom. That would be better at least. She wouldn't have to puke in front of everyone. She'd be by herself, safely in a stall, with some of her dignity still intact.

"I see a sign right down there. Women's restroom." Her kindhearted seat buddy patted Lauren's back and pointed. "Would you like me to go with you?"

Oh good heavens, no. Please just let me be. Lauren shook her head, offered a rushed "Thank you anyway," and took off for the women's restroom, still unsure that she'd make it that far. She closed in on the doorway, the rolling in her stomach warning of the impending mess to come.

A few more steps. Almost there. Just a few—

No!

A sign blocking the entry read *closed*, the passage webbed with yellow tape to emphasize the point. The bathroom was closed! How could it be closed? This was an airport—they needed a women's restroom. An *open* women's restroom!

It didn't matter. This was happening. Lauren was going to throw up, and she was going to throw up *now*.

She charged into the open door next to the women's restroom, which, of course, would be the men's. She didn't care. She needed a toilet and she needed her dignity and that was all. Rushing forward, she passed through the doorway only to smash flat into the crisp white shirtfront of a tuxedoed man.

"Whoa there." The low voice wafted above her head. "I think your headed in the wrong—"

Caught in the arms of a faceless stranger... Faceless because she couldn't muster the courage or the balance to look up.

Her stomach turned in one final lurch. And it happened. Right there on a stranger's dress shirt and suitcoat. Lauren threw up, discovering as she lost her late lunch, which included picante sauce, that, actually, throwing up in a crowded airplane wasn't the worst thing ever. Vomiting on a strange man in the doorway to the men's restroom was infinitely more humiliating.

Please let this be a nightmare. And let it be over now.

The prayer had barely rolled through her mind before Lauren heaved against the man yet again.

What a way to start her brand-new, glorious, independent life.

***

Not every day a guy walked from the bathroom, tossing the paper towel he'd been using toward the garbage, only to be slammed into by a sick woman in desperate need of...

Well, that about summed up his day.

Matt stared down at the small brunette losing the contents of her stomach against his rented tux. As much as he'd wanted to howl in frustration the whole day through, a surge of compassion melted the anxious stiffness from his arms. As she heaved against him a second time, he cupped the back of her head.

"Guess we've both had a rough day, huh?" he said quietly, his other hand bracing her shoulder.

"I'm..." Dry heave. "So..." Another false alarm. "Sorry."

Honestly, it could be worse. *Had* been worse, about three hours before. Given the choice between going back to stand with John, watching all his hopes and dreams change her name to his buddy's, or being puked on in the airport by a stranger, he'd take the vomit. Every single day.

Oddly, the tension in his jaw and shoulders eased. He stood there, holding a woman he'd had yet to properly meet, while the squall of her stomach worked itself out. Evidently, having a cute brunette puke down the front of you made for a decent distraction from life's massive disappointments.

When she went limp against him, her forehead pressed into his chest and warm nastiness oozing through both the dress shirt and his T-shirt, he trailed his hand down the waves of her hair and

Jennifer Rodewald

gave her a gentle squeeze. "Better?"

She moaned.

"Is there more?"

"I'm begging God right now that the answer is no. And also that Jesus would come right this second to take me home to some mansion in the sky. No more tears, no more sorrow. No more throwing up on men I've never met."

Matt chuckled. "A spotless white wardrobe does sound good right now."

Her groan quivered against his chest before she moved away. "I'm so terribly sorry. And embarrassed. Horrified, actually. I'll pay for the cleaning. Or a new suit. Whichever you prefer."

While she babbled, he caught the crimson staining her cheekbones, though she had yet to look up at him. Again, his heart pooled with sympathy.

He rubbed her shoulders and then squeezed. "This suit isn't a keeper anyway."

"What?" Finally she looked up at him. Big brown eyes, sheened with tears and exhaustion and humiliation, latched on to his. "Not a keep— Oh." Her eyes squeezed shut. "It's a rental, isn't it?"

"Yep."

"Oh no. I'm so, so sorry. I'll pay for it."

He'd never have believed he'd find a reason to laugh that day. Yet this woman—still nameless to him—managed to pull another chuckle from his muddied day. For that reason alone, he liked her on the spot.

"You know what?" He stepped back, taking in the red putrid mess on his front. "Don't worry about it." Meeting her eyes again, he enjoyed the easy feel of a smile relieving the tension that had made his jaw and cheekbones ache.

"No, really—"

He held up a hand. "No, I'm serious. After all, I got in your way. If I hadn't, you might have made it to the garbage can." He pointed to his right and behind him. "So it's my fault, I think."

"Oh my gosh." Both hands covered her face.

Stepping forward again, Matt tipped her chin up with a crooked finger. This personal encounter was new to him—he wasn't normally so...touchy. But. Well. But. He'd never been puked on, and he was pretty sure this miserably embarrassed soul hadn't ever vomited on a stranger before. That put them squarely together in the same boat of awkward firsts. Might as well try for comfort.

"Listen, it's not a thing, really," he said. "I'm just gonna grab my bag there and do a quick change. No big deal. Okay?"

One giant, break-his-already-severed-heart tear leaked onto the side of her nose. If he wasn't covered in vomit, he'd have pulled her into a full hug. Instead, he brushed the moisture trailing her face with the pad of his thumb. "Come on now. Don't cry."

"Okay." Another drop seeped from the corner of her eye and onto his thumb.

He chuckled. Again. That was three times. And he was charmed.

"Let me change, and then you can tell me your name."

Big brown eyes were watching him when he turned to retrieve the suitcase at his heels. As he rounded his way back into the bathroom, he hoped she'd still be around when he got done.

She'd likely not be, humiliated as she was.

He should have gotten her name.

Chapter Two

(in which Matt officially meets Lauren)

"Are you feeling better?"

Startled, Lauren looked up and then wanted to hide her face behind her hands. As soon as the man had disappeared into the men's room, she'd scurried away, crumpled onto one of the not-so-comfortable terminal chairs, slid into a ball, and tried to hide from the flurry of grounded passengers. After checking her earlier texts from the lodge where she was expected, and then checking in with the rental cars, followed by the road reports, she figured she might as well sit it out somewhere inconspicuous. She was not leaving the airport anytime soon.

She'd debated waiting around for the man who had caught her vomit to reappear from the bathroom. She really didn't want to face him again. On the other hand, she owed him something. Another apology, or fifteen thousand. A clean suit. Dinner. Something.

In the end, she opted for the cowardly route, which meant escaping while he wasn't present. Hoping that he would change his clothes and continue on his way, never, ever looking for the woman who'd ruined his rented tux by throwing up on him in the men's bathroom.

That was not to be, as the man, after apparently looking for her, lowered onto the seat two spaces away. He held out an unopened water bottle. "Still not feeling any better then, huh?"

"Thanks." She accepted the water as she pushed herself up from her slumped posture. "I'm okay now, I think. Not going to mess up your clean clothes anyway."

Trying for a smile, she forced herself to look at him. Of course she would've had to puke on a nice-looking man. One with kind brown eyes, a well-shaped jaw, a rather sharp nose, and a mouth whose narrow lips seemed prone to smiling.

She still didn't know his name. Just as well, as that way she could keep her anonymity.

"I was worried about you."

He was? He wasn't completely relieved that she'd disappeared, and good riddance?

"I thought you'd hang around and let me make sure that you were okay." He sat back and draped a casual arm onto the back of the chairs between them. "Instead, you disappeared. I didn't even know your name."

"You want to know my name?"

"Well, I think I should, considering all we've been through together."

A laugh peeked from behind her lingering embarrassment. "That's living dangerously. Who knows what will happen next."

He looked around the terminal and smiled. "Well, I could be stuck at an airport in the middle of a late-October blizzard."

"Yes. There is that, and you're welcome." She shook her head and sighed. "Everything is shut down."

He shrugged and crossed his arms. "There you have it. The worst has happened. You threw up on me, and now we're stuck at the airport together. So I probably should know your name."

"Lauren," she said. "My name is Lauren Matlock."

"Well, Lauren Matlock, welcome to the Lake Tahoe area. Unless you're returning home—in which case, welcome back."

She relaxed against the back of her chair. "No, this is my first time this far west."

"Ah. And what a welcome you've had." With a wink, he sat forward again and held out a hand. "I'm Matt. Matthew Murphy, and if you say my last name, you have to say my full first name—otherwise it sounds weird."

Shaking his hand, she scrunched up her nose. "Matt Murphy sounds weird?"

"Yes, but do not tell my mother. She'll argue with you about it. She likes alliterations. My father intervened after my birth, saving my brothers from the weirdness of an alliterated name, but I'm stuck with it. The extra syllable in Matt*hew* makes it bearable. So it's either Matt or it's Matthew Murphy, but not Matt Murphy."

Wide eyed and amused, Lauren gawked at him. "Matthew Murphy. Or just Matt. Got it. Anything else I should know?"

He tipped his chin upward, mocking a deeply thoughtful expression. "Not that I can think of at the moment." Then he snapped his fingers. "Oh! Except for I might be a tad hungry, and I'm guessing since you lost everything that was in your stomach, and if you're feeling better, you might be hungry too."

This time she laughed outright. "I'm not sure that I am. But I am sure I owe you at least some food, so what will it be?"

He got up, held out his hand to her, and then grabbed his rolling travel bag. Once again accepting his offered hand, she stood, situated her coat, which had been flung onto the arm of the chair, into the crook of one arm, and also settled her travel bag so she could pull it along behind her.

"I guess I'd probably better try to eat something."

"Right," he said, his hand now at her elbow. "So what will it be?"

"I asked you first."

"Second."

"I think you get to choose, given this very strange meeting that we've had."

Matt pointed down the terminal toward the food court at the end of the hub. "How about we just wander down there until we find something that looks at least halfway appealing to you?"

She nodded.

"So where are you from, Lauren Matlock?"

Falling into step beside him seemed easy, and their wheels

harmonized into a drag-clunk rhythm that complemented the click of her boots and the slap of his dress shoes against the tiled floor.

"Out east," she said.

"Out east?" One eyebrow cocked upward. "That's not very specific. Are you hiding?"

"No." She chuckled. "No, I'm not hiding. I'm just...well, maybe I'm seeking."

"Ah." He passed a glance that was curious and evaluative and still kind. "And what are you seeking, Miss Matlock?"

Indeed, what was she seeking? Independence? Self-acquaintance? Purpose? Maybe some of each, but also more.

Lauren drew a breath and paused in the middle of the movement of people all around them. What was she seeking? "My place in this world."

His grin, the one that had been friendly but maybe a bit of a mask, softened into something more serious and sincere. "Refreshingly honest." His voice lowered, and his gaze remained fastened. "And aren't we all?"

***

Matt leaned back in his chair, watching while Lauren pushed around the bottom fourth of her soup. At least she'd eaten something. Also, at least he wasn't stuck in this airport with only his disappointment and resentment to keep him company.

That was a little bit of a pity party. And actually, he technically wasn't stuck at all. He knew this area—knew the backroads, and he had a reliable four-wheel-drive vehicle that would get him anywhere he wanted to go. Probably. He was free to leave the airport at any time, as long as he stayed in the Lake Shores area.

He'd rather not. And he wasn't gonna go back to his childhood home—which was over two mountain passes away.

"Are you coming or going?" Lauren laid her soup spoon onto the plate, clearly giving up on the remainder of her chicken noodle soup.

"Going." Matt tried for a neutral tone. By the lift of her eyebrows, he'd missed.

"Where?"

Huh. Where, indeed? He'd known the gate number, because the lady at the desk had told him, and that was the only immediately pertinent information he'd needed. Likely, she'd given him a destination too, but he hadn't much cared or listened, not with the looping *get me out of here* plea that had saturated his mind at that time.

"Is it a secret? Are you like FBI or CIA or something?" Lauren leaned forward, mischief in her expression, warming to her teasing string. "Maybe your name isn't Matt at all. That whole *call me just Matt or Matthew Murphy* monologue was just a ruse to distract me from who you really are."

He stared at her, likely grinning, because she was definitely amusing. He leaned in and employed a low conspirator's voice. "Who am I?"

"Weston." She sat back and folded her arms smugly. "You're Michael Weston, and you're a spy. Burned. Searching for whoever sold you out while you were saving countless innocent people in daring acts of hero-esque intervention. You're trying desperately to regain your old job."

Matt snorted. "Done yet?"

"No. I'm onto you, mister."

This time he laughed. "You got me. I totally look like the guy in *Burn Notice*, so I have no idea why I thought I could get away with it."

As her arms slipped to her sides, Lauren giggled softly, and Matt liked the sound of it. More, he liked that on a day when he'd thought he'd rather dig his own grave than face the sunset, he was sitting across from an entertaining woman who had interesting down to a practiced art.

See. Not abandoned.

The small voice in his head hit him as much annoying as it was comforting. Probably because he was still mad at the One to whom it belonged. He banished such thoughts and smothered the voice, as neither were as amusing as this new friend.

"All right." Lauren sobered, her voice losing the movie-announcer quality she'd shifted into earlier. "Enough goofing around. Are you going to tell me where you were going all dressed up in a tuxedo, or are we destined to play twenty questions? Or worse, you're going to make me invent a story for you that will likely end in danger and misery, because I'm the tragic sort when it comes to fiction."

Wow. The woman had a surplus of words. Not that that was a bad thing, because still, she was diverting and a smidge on the side of hilarious.

Matt unzipped the side slot to his carry-on, searching for his boarding pass. Once found, he studied it and then turned to point down the terminal hallway they'd trekked twenty minutes before. "Gate B29. Looks like Miami."

"Seriously?"

He flipped the slip to face her. "That's what this says."

"No. I mean, seriously, you didn't know where you were going?"

As a tinge of heat brushed the tips of his ears, he shrugged, focusing his attention more than necessary on returning the unused boarding pass to the slot where it had come from.

"How is that possible?"

"I told the lady at the counter to get me on the first available flight out of Nevada. I guess Miami, flight 367, was it."

"Miami, as in Florida?"

"I think so?"

"You don't even know that?" With a crumpled brow, she stared at him like he was nuts.

Yeah. Maybe he'd been a little nuts. Wasn't exactly his fault though. Not knowing what to say, he shrugged.

"And the tux?"

So far Lauren had proven herself to be a fairly smart woman. She'd have him figured in less than ten seconds. That sensation that had been tickling his ears now burned, racing down his neck.

"Wait," she said.

Yep. She'd figured it out. Matt swallowed while he shifted in the chair. Maybe he'd just better start talking before she invented another tale that had the possibility of painting him as a villain. He'd much rather she think of him as a Michael Weston.

"I...left a wedding. Kind of in a hurry."

One eyebrow arched, giving Lauren's rather pretty face a sharp edge. "Why?"

"Because I didn't think I'd make it through the vows."

All traces of a smile faded as she nailed him with clear disapproval. "And it didn't occur to you to say something *before* the big day?"

"It did... but I thought I could do it."

"So you're a coward." She sat back, crossing her arms.

"That's not really fair."

"What kind of man leaves a girl on the day of their wedding?"

"Wait a minute! It wasn't *my* wedding."

Once again her eyebrows gathered and she leaned toward him. "Not your—you weren't the groom?"

"No."

And then clarity dawned as her mouth formed a silent *Ooo*.

Pathetic. Matt looked down at the table.

"I see," Lauren said, her voice now soft. "And I puked on you, to top it all off."

He moved his eyes to see her again, and a small chuckle left his chest. "Actually, that part wasn't so bad."

"I'm sorry." She reached across the narrow space between them, then her hand warmed his elbow. "Not about that. Well, actually, I *am* sorry about that—about the puking thing. I mentioned I was sorry, right?"

He nodded, that amusement she provoked overcoming his misery.

"But also, I'm sorry about the wedding, about seeing someone else marry her. That *was* it, right? The girl you loved married someone else?"

"Yeah. One of my best friends."

"Ouch."

Ouch didn't touch it, but he appreciated the sympathy.

Lauren waited a full ten seconds before she spoke again, which, guessing by the conversation they'd shared since the moment she'd overcome both her humiliation and travel sickness, was likely a record for her.

"How long after you broke up before he started to date her?"

"What?" His head came up.

Her chin tipped to one side, and she gazed at him like he was a lost puppy, starving and abused. "How long since you broke up with her?"

"I didn't..."

"What!" Her eyes flew wide with outrage. This woman couldn't possibly hide her emotions if the security of the nation depended on it.

"Katrine and I never dated." His face blazed, and he wished it wouldn't be completely pitiful of him to hide behind his hands like a small boy.

"Oh." As quickly as it had flared, her anger dissipated, and she slouched back again. "I...see."

Likely she did, which didn't make him feel any better.

Another brief lull settled, during which he tried to picture anything other than Katrine, all fancied up in her bridal elegance, stepping down that aisle. Toward him. And John. No, toward John and *not* him. He skipped the replay of the day and fast-forwarded to the moment he'd run into—literally—the talkative, interesting Ms. Lauren Matlock. Even if she had lost her lunch all over his shirtfront, that moment was a much more pleasant memory.

"So." Lauren broke through that small span of silence. "Miami, huh?"

Despite himself, one corner of his mouth quirked. Obviously, she couldn't help herself, and heaven bless her for that.

Chapter Three
(in which Lauren agrees to travel in a blizzard— with Matt)

"Let's pretend you had actually chosen Miami and the relocation wasn't some random cocktail of flight availability and an airline employee's whim." Lauren relaxed against the back of her chair, stirring her ice with her straw, compulsively lost in the curiosity of Matt Murphy—scratch that. Matthew Murphy, who apparently ditched a wedding in heartbreak.

And she'd thought *she* was running. "What do you think you'd do in Miami?"

Matt tipped his drink, sucking on the straw. The garbling sound indicated that there was nothing in the cup left to sip. After shaking the cup, he set it back down on the table and shrugged. "Sure I could find something."

While his lack of planning shouldn't have surprised her—after all, he hadn't even known where the plane he'd been scheduled to board was headed—Lauren stared at him as if his mind had been mushy.

"You could...find something?"

He shrugged again. "I grew up working with my dad—he builds custom sheds. And when I say *sheds*, I mean miniature mansions for people to house their lawn gear. So I'd find something."

"Huh." She tipped her head. "And where were you going to stay?"

"A hotel?"

"Is that an answer? Because it sounded more like a question. And if it's an answer, it's not a very good one. Do you know how financially uneconomical it is to *live* at a hotel?"

Matt's brow lifted. "Oh, you're a finance person?"

"No, and you still haven't answered my question."

"Not finance, but clearly a planner. I'll bet every square in your calendar app has at least three things listed in it."

She sealed her lips, refusing to play even if his banter was engaging.

"I'll also wager that you're never late. You're five minutes early for everything because if you're actually right on time, that's late in your book."

Staring at him, she continued saying nothing.

Matt laughed, stretching his hand, palm up, across the table. "Let me see your calendar."

"Not a chance, mister."

A mischievous gleam flashed in his eyes. "You owe me."

"I bought supper."

"Think that covers it? You did vomit on my rented tux, which I had to throw away."

"You said it wasn't a thing."

He made a tsk noise. "But you still felt bad."

"My guilt is appeased."

"Doubt it. It'll keep you up at night." Elbow on the table, he leaned his jaw against his palm. "You'll lie there thinking about how I gave you a chance to atone for all the putrid nastiness you inflicted on my suit, and you refused. And then the guilt will come back as a roaring beast, robbing you of sleep and peace and happi—"

"Okay!" Shaking her head, she rolled her eyes. "Sheesh, you're annoying. I've only known you for like an hour, and you're totally annoying. Where did you learn that level of annoyingness?"

Matt's grin spread like a champ's, a mix of charming boy and slightly devilish, as he sat back in a smug position. "Brothers. I have six brothers."

"Do they still claim you?"

"All but one. And believe it or not, I'm not the orneriest of the pack. Jackson has me beat, hands down." He wiggled his fingers at her. "Now hand it over."

"Fine." She slapped her cell onto his palm.

He clicked the Home button and then eyed her after the screen came to life. "Passcode?"

"As if I'd give that to a stranger."

"I'm not a stranger. You puked on me. We're bonded for life."

"Not gonna happen, Captain Confidence."

With a quick move, he slid his chair around the table and landed next to her. She sat back and to the side as he leaned into her space, bringing with him the scent of lemongrass and pine, which, she noted, was much better than vomit.

"Okay, Private Privacy, open it and then pass it back. We have a bet to see to."

She took back the phone and held her thumb on the screen, unlocking the machine and handing it back to him. "For the record, there's no bet in play here."

"Yes there is. I distinctly remember saying *I'll bet*."

"True. But I did not respond to that, so no bet."

His attention left her phone, now in his palm, and squared securely on her face. Heat filtered into her cheeks. Surely she wasn't blushing. Why would she blush? There was nothing to blush about. Just because this handsome, nice, amusing man was sitting close—as in invading her space close—and acting all charming. Didn't mean she should blush.

Heartbroken. Don't forget heartbroken on that list of Matt's personal attributes.

Exactly. Matt was a heartbroken soul. And she wasn't blushing.

"Now I'm curious, Ms. Matlock from somewhere out east. What brought you from out east to this far west?" The phone remained in his palm while he scrutinized her.

She remained determined not to blush. *For the love of dignity! Don't. Blush.*

"Aren't you going to check my phone?"

"In a minute. Answer the question."

"The screen will close in about ten seconds."

He glanced at the cell in his palm. "You have this timed in your head?"

"Doesn't everyone?"

Leaning out of her space—and thank goodness—he swiped the various app icons, tapped her calendar, and switched to month view for October. "Oh my. This is worse than I thought. At least three in every box—and this one!" He tipped the screen as if to show her but moved it back before she could see which date he was referring to. "This one has, like, twelve items. You are quite the busy girl, aren't you? Do you really think you can accomplish a week's worth of tasks in twenty-four hours?"

She doubted he was expecting her to answer, so she didn't.

After a pause, during which he glanced her direction, he moved on. "Let's see what we have going on today…"

Lauren shut her eyes and sighed. Not because she was irritated with Matt—he could look to his heart's content. She really didn't have anything to hide from him, a near stranger who had ditched a wedding that wasn't his because the bride belonged to someone else. Nope. Nothing for her to be bashful about on that calendar. The sigh came from…resignation. Literally and emotionally.

She'd resigned from her own sister's campaign. *Who does that?*

Worse, it had been a relief to do it—which made her feel guilty.

"Who is this Ashley person who monopolizes your time?"

Didn't take him long. "She's…running for state legislature."

Matt's raised-eyebrow gaze pinned back on her face. "Which state?"

"New Hampshire."

"And now I know…"

"Feel better?"

"Absolutely. If a girl is gonna puke on me, I should know from where she hails, don't you think?"

"Are you ever going to let that go?"

"Nope. Carrying it with me till death do we part."

He froze on that phrase, and she wondered why he chose those words specifically. Hopelessly stuck in his brain, likely. As his attention wandered, the mischievous set of his mouth and the gleam of orneriness in his eyes faded. Holding for several long moments, his silence tattled on the real state of his internal matters.

"She's really something, huh?" Lauren voiced the question softly.

The bob of his throat, the pressed line of his lips, and the way he blinked answered before he found the ability to speak again. "She was...my future. I thought."

"Did you ever tell her that?"

"No. Yes." The hand not holding her phone jammed through his hair. "I thought I did, but maybe not with words."

"Words are more understandable, you know?"

"Maybe. Always heard actions spoke louder."

"Well, she probably heard you loud and clear this time, leaving the wedding. Dressed as you were, I assume you were in the party?"

"Yeah." His voice cut harsh on that word. The faraway, sad expression slipped from his face, and he gave his head a slight shake. "Listen, your life is way more fun to talk about right now than mine. Can we go back to that?"

When his brown eyes connected with hers, she held his gaze. When his mouth eased back into something light and fun, she felt the mirror of his expression slip onto her face. And when he nudged her shoulder, she nudged him back.

And didn't blush.

"Yes, we can go back to that. But not to Ashley or her campaign for New Hampshire state representative."

"Fair enough. Let's see what we have for today..." Matt buried his face back into her phone, having kept the screen alive with a rhythmic tapping of his thumb. "Ash...nah. That's taboo. Meeting with Dad. How'd that go?" He glanced at her.

Awkward. "Fine."

He nodded, then turned back to item number three on the list. "Arrive at Lake Shore Lodge." Again, his head bobbed up, and he sat straighter. "Lake Shore Lodge? That's your destination?"

"Yes." She bit her lip, taming her amusement at his enthusiasm.

"I know that place! It's kind of awesome, right off Tahoe. Dad had several builds for the resort. A carriage house for the horse-drawn buggy and sleigh. A giant gazebo. And I think a cabin, if I remember right."

"I thought you said he built sheds?"

"*Custom* sheds. Which easily convert to those kinds of projects. Dad's the best. Pretty well known around the North Shores region actually."

"Huh." She pictured the brochures she'd pored over. Loved. Had recently made a mental exercise of often imagining herself in those pictures as a stress-relief remedy. Walking the mist-dusted trails, the colors of fall and evergreens surrounding her. Paddling on the cool waters of the lake, which lay within walking distance of the lodge. Sitting in that gazebo that Matt's dad apparently had built.

"When are you going?" Matt intruded on her slip into dreamworld.

Lauren came back to the present, and at his question, checked her Fitbit. "I was supposed to be there by now." A warm palpitation strummed against her chest. *Late.* A four-letter word. One she avoided—both saying and practicing. But there she was—late. And she'd become so distracted that she hadn't even called the lodge owner!

So irresponsible! And you're supposed to be his new director of guest activities? Mr. Appleton will fire you before you even begin.

This was punishment. Retribution for her abandoning her sister in the tender beginnings of Ashley's bid as the state's youngest legislative representative.

How could you, Laurs? I need your type A in this. Who is going to keep my insane schedule straight?

The hard strumming of her heart met the accompaniment of

scalding acid in her stomach. Lauren loved her sister. Underneath the layers of frustration and—yes—resentment, she did love Ashley. But the sourness in her own spirit had become more than she could live with, and after praying through nearly a year of that bitterness, Lauren felt the distinct need to step out from the weighted shadow of her family and all the expectations that came with being a Matlock in New Hampshire.

She didn't want to abandon anyone. But she did want a life. Her own, redefined. Whatever that meant.

"Lauren?" Matt snapped his fingers near her hand, where she'd been staring.

"I'm late," she whispered, horrified. "I've failed, and I haven't even started."

"Failed?" He laughed, leaned back, and dropped a friendly arm around her shoulders. "There's a blizzard out there, remember? Pretty sure Mr...." That arm that had plopped over her lifted, and he tapped his head with her phone. "Oh come on! Mr....it was a fruit, right?" He looked at her as if she could supply the answer.

"Appleton?"

He snapped again. "That's it. Mr. Appleton. He's a good'un. Always supplied us with lunch at the lodge and gave me root beer on the house. Big deal for a kid, you know?"

"Okay..."

"Right. Pretty sure he understands about a blizzard. Just call him."

She leveled him with a deadpan look. "I would, but I seemed to have lost my phone."

And there it was again. That smile. "Right."

His fingers brushed hers as he passed her cell back into her possession so she could make the call.

She didn't blush then either. Probably. She did get up and move across the half-populated airport restaurant to find a quiet place to make her call. That way, just in case, Matthew Murphy wouldn't suspect the color warming her face had anything to do with him at all.

After all, he was heartbroken. And she wasn't looking for that kind of redefinition anyway.

***

Matt slouched against the back of the chair, wrung out. This day had been...

Not as bad as it had started out, actually. The ache still knotted, but as he watched Lauren weave her way toward an empty place where she could call Mr. Appleton, a gentle ribbon of gratitude soothed some of the worst sores.

You sent her to puke on me, didn't You? Clever, Lord. But thanks. She's a...happy distraction from the disappointment.

Honestly, he'd rather God not have let him plunge into this Death Valley level of disappointment in the first place. Hadn't he prayed daily—almost hourly—for intervention on John and Katrine's wedding? More, hadn't he petitioned since he'd been twenty years old for Katrine's undivided heart?

This, it seemed, was the divine answer. Snowbound in an airport with a woman in distress. She was an interesting woman in distress though. Quick witted, fun to talk to. And like he'd thought before, a happy distraction. So yes, he was thankful for that. And also, he could help her out of this trapped-at-the-airport thing, because who really wanted to spend longer in an airport than necessary?

The thoughts produced a plan in his head as Lauren finished her phone call and turned back toward him with a look of both relief and misery—the latter likely because, heaven forbid, Miss Perfectly Punctual was late and there was nothing for it—and slowly made her way back to their table. Call it male ego or whatever, but the thought of stepping in for the rescue sat kind of nicely on his battered self-worth, and he gripped that burgeoning plan with every shred of dignity he had left.

"Well?" he asked as she lowered into her chair again.

She sighed. Relief. And defeat. "I'm not fired, at least."

"Pshh." He waved his hand. "He wasn't even upset, was he?"

"Well." She peered into the crowd, as if imagining the man's face, trying to find a trace of a scowl. "No, actually. He wasn't."

"And this surprises you."

"Uh."

"The thing is, Miss Neat and Orderly, you're walking into a fairly relaxed gig. Lake Shore is awesome, but it's not the Plaza. So breathe. It's gonna be fine."

She glanced at him. He wasn't sure if the gleam in her eye was irritation or appreciation. He opted to believe it was appreciation and plunged ahead with his rescue-the-damsel plan.

"Also, here's more good news." Sitting up, he grinned. "I can get you there."

"What?"

"To Lake Shores." He pulled out his keys from his jeans pocket. "I can get you there."

"You—no, you can't." One slim hand came up and closed over his, pushing his key-clasping fingers away. "In case you didn't understand the implications of *blizzard* and *everything shut down*, the roads are closed."

"I have a four-wheel drive."

"Roads. Closed."

"Just the highways."

"Are you insane?"

"No. I don't have certification to verify that though."

"I thought you were leaving Nevada, anyway."

"I am. With you. Lake Shore is just across the state line." He moved to stand. "Let's go."

"What makes you think I'm going anywhere in a blizzard with a recently heartbroken man whom I really know nothing about? I am *not* crazy."

"Would it help if I told you I'm a Christian?"

"You're—" Her lips closed suddenly, and her brow folded inward. With an intensity that rivaled a rocket scientist calculating a launch, she studied his face.

"Are you actually looking for Jesus?" he said.

"It'd help." She continued her examination. "Don't you think? It'd be very helpful if the seal of the Holy Spirit was something all believers could see. Like a mark of the brotherhood or something?"

A laugh burst from his mouth. "That would be nice, I guess. Pretty sure the only mark I've read in the Bible wasn't a good one though."

Her scrutiny turned suspicious. "What's your favorite verse?"

"Joshua 1:9. 'Be strong and of good courage. Do not be afraid, do not be discouraged, for the LORD your God will be with you wherever you go.'"

The pinched expression relaxed as she fought against the smile tilting one side of her mouth. "Mildly impressive."

Crossing his arms, he mimicked her earlier doubtful pose. "And you, Miss Testify, what is yours?"

The sass that had made her eyes gleam dimmed, and she moved her attention to her hands. Matt sucked in a breath against the piercing sensation that he'd accidently poked at something tender.

"It has changed a few times over the years. The seasons of life, you know?" Her far-off look came back to land on him. "But right now the words I cling to are from Isaiah 49. It says, 'I will not forget you. See, I have engraved you on the palms of my hands.'"

Powerful words for a heart tossed into a lonely wilderness. A sudden, bizarre need to gather this woman close and hold her against his chest swept over Matt, bringing questions along as well. Why would he do that? She was a stranger. Must be that knight impulse he'd just been feeding. Or perhaps the revelation of a mutual ache.

Bad idea. He smothered the whim. That particular move would likely not be appreciated.

He did lean toward her though. "That's a pretty sweet promise."

"Yeah." She met his eyes, and for a quiet moment they held there, as if understanding tied them together. With a small closed-mouth smile, she nudged his shoulder.

"So." His voice garbled a bit. He cleared his throat and moved back toward the shallower end of this budding friendship. "Do I pass?"

"Are you really a believer?"

"I am. Saved by grace. Born again. Sealed by the Holy Spirit. And as a related side note, my mother worked really, really hard to raise her boys to be gentleman. With seven of us, you can imagine that took quite an effort. She might be a saint, but I'm not sure. My church doesn't go into that."

That provoked a chuckle and a headshake, and then she stood. "And what about the closed roads?"

He shrugged. "I thought you were from New England. Doesn't it snow in New England?"

"Yes. But when there's a blizzard"—she motioned toward the large window across the terminal—"I heed the advisory not to drive in it."

He tipped his head. "Do you always do as you're advised?"

She drew back, wariness in her look, visibly withdrawing that fledgling trust he'd just sought.

Bad move. That sounded... He wasn't sure what it sounded like. A dare? If so, she wasn't biting. Matt abandoned the joking and put on genuineness. "I know this area really well. I can get you there safely. I promise."

Chapter Four
(in which Matt and Lauren travel in a blizzard)

Twice in one day. As in, this current jostling through a road that legitimately should be *closed* was display number two that she was insane.

Lauren clutched the grab on the truck door, her grip so rigid that a cramp shook her forearm. *Backroads* meant everything the word implied, and worse. Actually, *road* seemed to be an overly generous term. The trail Matt's truck cut through the snow was marked only by the towering evergreens lining either side of the waves of heavy white drifts blanketing what she assumed was the road beneath.

Could he really and truly know where he was going in this wild sea of shifting white?

"This was a bad idea." She spoke through clenched teeth.

Hunched over the steering wheel, concentration etched into every muscle, Matt pretended to grin. Pretended, she was sure, because the one corner of his mouth that attempted a lift remained more puckered than easy. "I'll get you there. Promise."

Yeah, that helped. Drawing in a deep breath meant to ease the knotting of her core, she refocused on what Matt claimed to be a road. "Should I pray?"

"Couldn't hurt. That's what I've been doing."

"Awesome." What had she agreed to? What had she been thinking?

This time the shift of his lips created something closer to an actual grin. "It's an adventure. I assume that's what you left home and family for, right?"

"Uh, sure. Adventure."

"No?"

"Yes."

"I'm not convinced."

"You're driving. Sort of." She waved toward the largely obscured white trail ahead of them. "You need to focus."

"I'm zeroed in on the road, little Ms. Nervous Enough for the Both of Us. Don't you worry about that."

Who started this name thing they had going? "Okie dokie. Not a care in the world over here. Just bouncing through a blizzard."

"You're not going to throw up again, are you?"

Lava crept against her chilly cheeks, and she was glad he needed to concentrate on keeping them between the trees. "Thought we weren't going to bring that up."

"No promises. I distinctly remember saying no promises on that one."

Slumping back against the seat, she groaned. "Ugh. This *was* a really bad idea."

Matt chuckled. "You can. Puke, I mean. I won't get mad. It was just a question so I could be prepared. Remember, I have a herd of brothers. There's likely nothing you could do that would freak me out."

Ha! The male population continued to underestimate their female counterparts. Nothing new under the sun. "No sisters?"

He hesitated, flickered a glance her way.

"Eyes on the road, buddy."

"Right." His head bobbed once. "No sisters. Just...one sister-in-law. Recently."

Was that hesitation in his voice? Interesting. She tucked the questions budding in her mind away for later and concentrated on the topic at hand. "Then I'm sure there are several female things I could toss at you that would totally freak you out." Not that she would, because how embarrassing would that be?

"Nah."

Hmm. Maybe worth the mild humiliation. She *had* puked on him and survived. Oh, so tempting... "Shall we bet on it, Mr. So Sure of Himself?" The name thing might be witty. Maybe that had been her invention. A clever one, and wasn't she smart? *How about that, Ashley? I am not entirely socially inept.* Swift as the thought came, she erased it. Ashley had never accused her of such a thing. She simply didn't include her in anything that was not academic, and later, campaign related. The sting of which...

Enough. New life, new attitude.

The stall of silence continued between them. Huh. Mr. Girls Can't Phase Me might be rethinking his position.

"Is this a long-term commitment?" Matt blurted, ending the telling space of quiet he'd let go.

Long-term com— Whoa. *What?* Shock nearly came off her lips, if not for the choking cough that caught the words in her throat.

"I mean this move," Matt interjected quickly, a touch of panic in his voice. "The job—is it long term? That's what I was talking about. Not..." He waved a hand in the space between them.

Lauren snorted and rather relished the color that crawled suspiciously up his neck, toying with his ears and threatening invasion on his cheeks.

Who could understand the mind of men? Flying places without a clue as to where they'd land. Driving through blizzards when *Road Closed* told reasonable humans to stay out of their cars and off the snow-drifted byways. And changing subjects without warning. Not to mention, rather conveniently. The scaredy-pants.

"Yes." Lauren tucked away her amusement for later use, certain there would be a *later use*. "The job is long term. I think." Hoped. Didn't have any other plans at the moment. She'd wanted to find out what life would be like if her time and her ambitions and her talents were put toward something she wanted. Something she found delight in. Perhaps that had been selfish. But living with resentment...

Turning away from that pathway of thought. Didn't need to go there, to submit to that emotional tug-of-war. The turmoil of it during the previous months had her on ulcer medication.

New life. New attitude.

"That's good," Matt said. "I mean, I think you're going to like the Lake Shore Resort. Like I said, it's a neat place. And Mr. Appleton is a good man. He'll be kind to you. Fair, I mean."

Was Matt babbling? Flirting, then babbling...huh. Mr. Bold and Confident feeling a touch...hmm, what? Shaky?

Of course he was. He was still brokenhearted. Bold and confident would seem like a good shield against hurt and humiliated, wouldn't it?

As Lauren moved compassion over the place that had bloomed with a greedy hope that Matt *had* been flirting, the corridor of tall pines closed in on them. Matt braked, cranking the wheels left. The unexpected turn put them into a slide right, the force pushing Lauren against her door. Shutting her eyes, she squealed.

A deep laugh interrupted her panic.

"We're fine," Matt said.

"Is this normal to you?"

A bounce of his shoulders and lift of his cheeks sufficed for his answer. Then, "I grew up in the hills. Don't worry. I can handle it. Three more turns, if I remember right. Then, my lady, I will have fulfilled my vow."

"I think you're nuts."

"Why, thank you."

"Uh. Sure?"

The forest blocked their forward path again, and this time the switch in directions tossed her toward him. Though her seat belt kept her in her seat, her upper body went with the motion, and she found her face pressed against his shoulder.

There was that lemongrass and pine smell again. Quite a nice scent.

Matt's glance down toward her face held laughter. "Unsteady

on the seas there?"

With both palms, she pushed against his solid arm—not that she noticed it was solid—and righted herself. "You're doing that on purpose."

"Just following the road."

Indeed. This was really a bad idea. Though that moment just now, snugged against his arm?

Maybe not so bad after all.

***

Matt breathed a silent sigh after the truck slid into the spot he'd aimed for and then settled. Almost right where he'd planned to park, with maybe a four-foot skid. Not bad, considering how slick the roads and then Lake Shore Resort's parking lot were. Honestly, he'd underestimated this storm. Severely.

The car settled into non-motion, and after a moment, Lauren leaned forward, wonder overriding the tension that had clamped her jaw. Her mouth parted and eyes sparkled as she took in the lodge and the surrounding forest waiting just beyond the windshield.

The tension in his arms and chest unfurled as he watched her take in the view. He sat back, unbuckled, and gave her a few moments to relish this new beginning.

Thank You, God, for the safety. For Lauren's sake—not sure she would have forgiven me for a wreck.

Maybe she would have though. Seemed to be a fairly easygoing woman, which hit him as odd, considering the filled-to-the-edges planner he'd inspected at the airport, and her very-apparent type A personality.

He knew that type. At least, he'd known *one* of that type. Had been in love with a woman of that type...

Nope. None of those thoughts. Katrine is blissfully wed, and God has smacked me with a distraction.

Should he really be thinking about Lauren as a distraction? At best, that was...demeaning. At worst, well, at worst it sounded immoral—which had not been what he'd meant at all.

No. No more thinking of her as a distraction. She was simply a woman who needed help, and he'd been happy to lend it.

"You look"—he leaned forward, hooking an elbow on the steering wheel to peer at her face—"captivating." No. Wait. Wrong word. Or wrong form of the right word. "Captivated. That's what I meant." *Down, heat.* The rush steaming up his neck did not comply.

Lauren barely glanced at him. Didn't seem to notice his slip. "It's enormously gorgeous." She gripped the dashboard, scooching forward on the seat.

With an almost silent chuckle at her description, Matt turned to look at the lodge and beyond again, delighting in her delight. "Surely there's enormously gorgeous places out east?"

"I'm sure there are. I lived in a city though, and business rarely allowed for an escape."

"Seriously?"

"This is amazing."

Had she not heard him? Maybe didn't want to get into it. She had flown all the way across a continent to start a new life.

Matt turned to open his door, hopped out, and slip-slid his way around the nose of his Ford, making it to her side as she popped open her door. He caught the edge, held it, and offered a gloved hand toward her.

"Here we are, Ms. Enormously Gorgeous." Holy smokes. He did it again! What was he thinking?

Lauren eyed him, smirked, and then accepted his hand.

So they skipped his slipup. Again. *And thank you, heaven.* "Let's get you into this slice of awesome, shall we?"

Her hand in his, she beamed up at him. Pleasure moved from his gut throughout his core at the pure, unfiltered delight in her expression. Simple joy provoked by the wonder of creation. A reaction he could understand. A delight he could easily share—and wasn't it nice to meet a woman who would react that way to the woods? The easy feeling that had slipped into the broken places within acted as a balm to a few more jagged edges as he walked beside Lauren, now holding her elbow as they picked their way around snow drifts and icy patches.

Up the stairs, which held more grip with the gritty finish on the risers—something common to this part of the world—and across the wide, covered front porch, they walked side by side into the two-story log lodge. The double doors had been fashioned from heavy wood, inset with one large pane in each, and opened on well-oiled hinges. At their feet, a large rug covered the tiled entry, which then transitioned into gleaming pinewood flooring, the polish of which was flawless. A fire crackled bright and cheery in the massive stone fireplace on the left end of the large, open front entry. On their right, a granite-topped counter, supported by a stone-covered pedestal, spread in front of a bank of six-paned windows. The front desk.

As warmth enveloped them—the closed doors now shielding exposed skin from the wind's bite and snow's sting—Lauren relaxed at his side.

"Out in this?" A deep voice drew attention to a pair of booted feet that eased down the wide front stairs. Wood railing flanked both sides of the risers, and a wide red carpet, appearing to have been recently vacuumed, tamped the sound of the large man's steps. "And what would incite a smart-looking young couple out into the wind and snow on this day?"

Matt dropped his hand. Lauren stepped forward. "We're not..." She fumbled over words as they spilled from her mouth too quickly. "I mean, we're out here together, but not a...well." She snapped her lips shut, lifted her spine straight, and fixed a professional smile. "I'm Lauren Matlock. Would you happen to be Mr. Harold Appleton?"

Matt stepped forward, touching her shoulder, because though she was clearly uncomfortable with the assumption the man— who Matt knew to be the very one she was looking for—had made, he couldn't help but be entertained by her stumbling for words.

He *was* a tease. His mother had warned him about that all through high school. *Don't tease the girls. They'll take it wrong, Matt, and that's not fair...*

Why that warning blipped through his mind, he couldn't say.

"Mr. Appleton." He reached out as he stepped forward, meeting the six-foot, nearly two-hundred-pound fellow with a handshake.

Harold Appleton studied him, and within three seconds, had found the match. "Ah. One of the Murphy boys. Matt, right?"

"Yes, sir."

"The oldest. Likes to build. And be outside. Should be mid-twenties by now?"

Impressive. Though the older man walked like the years were hard on him, his mind was ever sharp. "You've got it."

Appleton slapped him on the shoulder. "And how is it, Matt Murphy, that you've stumbled into this lodge with my newest employee in tow?"

Matthew Murphy. Or just Matt. Not Matt Murphy. This name really shouldn't bother him, should it? A man of twenty-six should have outgrown the need to correct these trivialities.

"I threw up on him."

Matt whipped around, catching the horror in Lauren's wide brown eyes as she smacked her lips shut. Apparently, by that careless admission, she still struggled with an embarrassment about her and him being a couple. He tucked his emerging grin near his shoulder, trying not to laugh as her face tinged a warm pink.

"I mean, at the airport. I got sick, and he got in my way, and it ended up messy..." One hand lifted, covering her mouth. Shutting her eyes, she shook her head. "This is not coming out right."

Appleton laughed, the sound of it far from soft or quiet. The fire seemed to grow in his amusement as it danced and flickered. Lauren peeked at Matt, a silent plea for help in her expression.

"Lauren got sick on the plane, which was stuck out on the tarmac, rocking in the wind while they waited for a gate to open. She tried to make it to the restroom once they deplaned, but the women's room was closed, and I got in her way when she bolted for the men's."

"And you'd never met before?" Appleton asked.

"Not once. Quite an introduction, right?"

"Let's not ever bring it up again, okay?" Though sounding a touch miserable, Lauren stopped hiding behind her hands.

"Good luck on that one, Ms. Matlock. The Murphy boys are as ornery as they are good looking."

Matt's turn to wash in embarrassment.

Appleton moved forward again, toward the counter. "All that being interesting, though, I do not understand why you are standing in this lodge and not waiting safely at the airport as we discussed nearly two hours ago."

The edge in his rebuke was more fatherly than disapproving, but it still poked against Matt's conscience. He moved to catch up to Appleton. "That would be my fault, sir. I promised Lauren I could get her here."

"In this?" One meaty hand motioned toward the sheets of white blowing outside.

"Uh, yeah. I might have underestimated the storm."

"How long was the drive?"

Matt glanced at Lauren, feeling about sixteen years old. "We left shortly after Lauren called you."

"Huh." Appleton rounded the granite counter and nailed a lifted-eyebrow look dead on Matt's face.

"How long is the drive on a good day?" Lauren stepped beside Matt, folding her hands on the counter now separating them from the lodge owner.

"Thirty minutes. Tops."

So much for that rescuing-the-damsel thing.

"I knew that had been a bad idea." She shoved him, the touch more playful than irritated.

"We made it," Matt said.

"On a prayer."

Mr. Appleton's booming laughter filled the whole of the lodge again. "Well, bless heaven for that, anyway. Glad you're safe." He waved them toward a glass-enclosed room that sat empty just beyond the front desk, hobbling toward it with a gait that looked painful. "Come on and get some hot cocoa, and we can talk beside the fire. The lodge is empty for the time, and by the weather forecast, we'll be slow for a couple of days. Might be good timing for you to start after all."

They followed, and Appleton pointed toward mugs and a canister labeled *Cocoa*. Lauren slipped out of her coat and hung it on a rack just outside the small breakfast nook's door and then accepted a prepared mug from Matt. He followed her lead and hung up his own coat, slipped out of his boots, and retrieved a mug of creamy chocolate, joining Mr. Appleton and now Lauren on a chair near the fireplace.

Stress seemed to peel off Lauren in layers, and as it did, she lost her propensity to babble. Mr. Appleton explained what he needed her to do in the coming weeks, her responsibilities going beyond a typical event planner.

"My wife ran this place with love and efficiency. It was her dream, and I can't stand the thought of it falling apart." A note of pain clipped his voice.

Hadn't heard about Mrs. Appleton's passing, but seeing the evidence of loss weaken the joy in Appleton's eyes blistered Matt's heart.

"I'm sorry she isn't here to see it done correctly, Mr. Appleton." Lauren sat straight while she talked. Clearly practiced at professional engagements. But her tone held genuine sympathy. Seemed like something rare.

"Ah." Appleton cleared his throat. "She gave me forty years of love and happiness. I miss her, but heaven bless it, I can't say that I wish her back. There are so many worse ways to make an exit. I'm glad hers was quick and not agonizing. And—" He braced the armrests of his chair. "She left behind a heart full of memories and a working dream to see me through to the end." He stood, then reached for Lauren's hand, which she accepted as she stood as well. "I'm glad you made it in safely, in spite of Matt Murphy." A wink fell toward Matt. "Your room is up the back stairs, first door on the right. I'm in the living quarters behind the breakfast nook—the hallway that leads to the kitchen. Knock if you need anything. Get settled tonight, and we'll sort out the rest tomorrow."

"That sounds good. Thank you, Mr. Appleton."

The man turned toward Matt. "And you?"

"Yeah, me..."

"Don't you dare try to go out in this. The Emerald Cove room is clean. Up the stairs, first door on the left. Take it for the night."

He left a few more instructions about food and then padded down a wide hall toward his living quarter. Matt retrieved the luggage from his truck, darkness making movement through the driving snow even more harried. After a quick supper of canned soup and a quiet sit in front of the fire, Lauren took herself to bed, leaving Matt alone to consider the day.

It'd been a long one. Seemed he'd lived two different lives in one day. How should he move forward from there? Miami had been a foolish impulse—this blizzard might just be God's intervention on his irrational compulsion. Hurt, disappointment, and anger had blinded him. Much of the anger part, if he were being honest, had been arrowed at God.

Squeezing his eyes shut, he allowed the image of Katrine as she'd caught him in the hall before the ceremony. *Tell me I'm doing the right thing*, she'd said. The interior of his mouth had taken on qualities of Death Valley as he'd stared at her. *I love John*, she'd continued. Arrows straight in his gut. *I should marry John.* He continued to say nothing while he sank beneath the sands of nauseating pain. *Matt?* Oh, she actually expected him to answer?

I can't make your choices.

That was what he'd said. Final words between them before she became Mrs. John Bently.

A sharp pain twisted in his chest. He wasn't positive who bore the most blame for it. Katrine, for toying with him. Again. *She doesn't mean to...* The same defense he'd covered her with for the past five years. Or himself, for being a coward. Again.

Tipping his head against the back of the leather sofa, he sighed. Then banished all thoughts of Katrine. Instead, he intentionally replayed the moment he met—caught—Lauren. And every silly incident involving her after that.

Lauren's sudden appearance in his world was the warm, gentle breeze that lifted from the valley after a harsh blizzard back home. She was the soft yellow ray of sunshine poking through dark storm clouds after a fierce spring rage. She was a lazy snowfall on a quiet winter's night.

And in the midst of a pain he'd prayed desperately for God to prevent, Matt was thankful.

Not forgotten.

Maybe so. Either way, he was thankful for a new friend.

Chapter Five
(in which Matt and Lauren are friends)

Spotting Matt coming down the wide staircase, Lauren turned away from the large front room with her phone pressed securely against her ear, giving him her back.

"I got here all safe and sound. No worries." Warmth pressed against her cheeks. Not because she lied. Well, maybe because she wasn't being exactly honest—there was that tiny issue of a blizzard shutting everything down. She did get stuck at the airport, technically. But technically, she did get to the lodge safe and sound. Thanks to Matt.

"I'm glad you're good." Ashley's tone indicated a clear *but* in that statement. "When we heard the airports were all shut down that way, and a sudden early blizzard hit harder than anyone expected, well, you can guess how we all were worried."

They were? That was nice and maybe a bit of a surprise. Perhaps Lauren had underestimated how much value she really had in her family—value that went beyond her ability to schedule efficiently and keep everyone on task.

"So..." Ashley's hesitation to move forward smothered that budding gratification of being appreciated for more than her secretarial skills. *Here it comes.* Lauren just knew it. "Things at the lodge are..."

"They're good, Ash." Lauren smiled big, hoping that the

expression carried through in her voice. Also, she needed the expression as she pivoted toward the sound of footsteps approaching her back. Certainly the footfalls belonged to Matt, and she wasn't ready to explain who Ashley was without at least two cups of coffee flowing through her system. "Everything is working out well here. Listen though." She met Matt's eyes as he came within three steps of the front desk, behind which she stood. His brows lifted, as for a moment he seemed to pause, but then his easy, ever-ready grin lifted the corners of his mouth and he sent her a small wave. She nodded at him. "I've got to go. First day and everything. There's a lot to learn, and I need to get to it."

"Okay. But—"

No. No *buts*. She could slip in a quick *I have a guest* and hang up. Except, though Matt had switched his direction from the front desk to the front door, he was still in earshot. Explaining a lie and Ashley all in one conversation, and without that necessary coffee, didn't seem like a great way to start the day.

Lauren stifled a sigh. "What's up, Ashley?"

"The thing is, Lauren, I've been thinking all of this through—you leaving. I really don't think it's a good idea."

That muted sigh came out in full measure. "We've talked about this."

"I know. But not much. I mean, you gave me all of two weeks' notice. What are you doing, sis? I mean, your family is here, and we need you. *I* need you."

With pressed lips, Lauren peered out the large paned window, watching as Matt gripped a shovel and clambered down the front steps. For a man whom she'd labeled *heartbroken* the day before, he sure seemed to move with a lightness she'd never known and was starting to envy. How much coffee had he consumed before he came down those stairs?

Lauren leaned her back against the high paneling of the front desk. "Ashley, you don't need me. And while it's nice that you want me, I feel like I need to find my own stride. Run my own race."

"Your own race?" Her sister's tone bit with offense. "Like

politics? Is that what this is about? You're mad that I'm running for the house? I never knew you wanted—"

"No." She covered her head with her palm. *Not ever.* "I don't want anything to do with politics. That's what I've been trying to tell you. Your career—I'm glad you're going for it. Glad you're excited. I'm hoping for the best for you. But that's what it is—yours. Your bid for representative isn't for me, Ashley. And to be honest, I'm afraid that if things continued the way they were, I'd never find what *is* for me."

The lack of response from the other end of the continent hung heavy against her, making the room feel much bigger—and emptier—than it had a moment before. Lauren shut her eyes, fought against a dizzying wave of guilt and frustration, mixed with a heavy dose of confusion.

Maybe she'd been selfish. Honestly, she couldn't say for sure.

The sound of scraping pulled her attention back outside. Matt settled into a rhythm of work as he shoveled the front walk. Again, she wondered at his ultra-fast rebound. She'd expect a man who'd witnessed the marriage of a woman he loved to be more sullen. Then again, that quick dive into work might be therapy.

People quite often simply kept moving, doing what they had to do. Which was exactly why she was there.

***

Matt had caught the bare bones of Lauren's phone conversation as he'd walked across the polished wood floor of the vaulted front room. He also did not miss the strain in her smile, nor the worried look in her eyes. Not to mention her use of the name *Ash*. As in Ashley, whom Lauren didn't want to speak of yesterday. Something was up with that woman, and it bothered him more than it should.

Skip it. Wasn't his business, not at the moment anyway. Matt had lifted a grin and a small wave toward Lauren and then altered his direction so that his steps would carry him out the front door.

The sun fought through the gauzy clouds, revealing a backdrop of blue behind the wispy remnants of the storm. Wind that had blown furious the night before now stirred the chilly morning air with the gentleness of a lamb. With his face upturned to soak in the determined warmth of the morning sun, Matt stepped off the wide front porch, snow shovel in hand.

First item: clear a path from the gravel lot to the deck—which would also need to be scooped clean. Next, he'd locate the wood pile to restock the half-full supply he'd spied near the giant stone fireplace inside. After that, he'd search out Mr. Appleton to see what else needed done—with the additional hope of a fruitful conversation.

Surely there was something for a recently unemployed twenty-six-year-old man to do around the lodge. Mr. Appleton had moved with all the agility of a rusty chain the night before. If he were to guess, Matt would say arthritis was being unkind to the nearly seventy-year-old man. If Matt could make a respectful case for the lodge's need of a strong back, work-worthy shoulders, and young legs, he might be golden. That was, depending on what Lauren thought of his dawning plan.

She might think he was a creeper. Or, perhaps more probable, pathetic. Running, in truth, was pathetic.

But he wasn't running. Maybe sort of hiding, but not running. Not like Miami had been. Working at the lodge would be more like finding a better fit for himself. Numbers on a spreadsheet had never been his thing. Nor had a suit and tie, not to mention a crowded office. Working with his hands, spending his days outdoors, breathing in pine-scented air, these all suited him much better than any bank job ever could have.

And the reason he'd even considered trying to make himself fit that other mold was now another man's Mrs.

Why not start over here, at the lodge? Grunt work suited him just fine, thank you very much.

Scrolling through possible ways to approach the topic with both Lauren and then Mr. Appleton, Matt settled into a rhythm of work. Scrape, scrape, scrape. Toss. The heavy slush landed with a plop on what Matt assumed was grass beneath a blanket of white.

As a cool band of sweat beaded near his hairline and his lungs expanded with the crisp, cool breath of purpose, scented by forest and lake, his confidence grew.

Hoping Appleton had a job for him definitely was not running. And actually it felt a whole lot like breaking free.

***

"You're still here." Lauren shifted her weight to her heels, widening the space Matt had closed when he leaned against the guest-services counter. Coffee now a strong presence in her system, and a solid two hours past her conversation with Ashley, had her in a better frame of mind.

Didn't hurt that seeing him felt a bit like an anchor of familiarity in a scene that was otherwise all new.

A lazy, though maybe sheepish-in-a-relaxed-sort-of-way, grin split the whisker-shadowed union of his lips, giving him a hint of mountain-man appearance. He smelled of cold outdoors, though he'd shucked his heavy coat long before he'd come back inside. A dark-blue flannel button-down served as his only protection against the near-freezing temps outside, and even that he'd rolled the sleeves to his forearms.

"I wanted to be sure to leave things better than I found them."

"Smart."

"Thank you." One hand clutched his coffee, fingers so long they nearly met around the circumference of the paper hot cup. The opposite hand rested on the countertop, fingers lightly drumming the granite of the counter that acted as a barrier between them. "Appleton put you to work already, I see."

She glanced at the computer screen she'd been staring at. Mr. Appleton had shown her around the inside of the lodge, gone over the things he'd hoped she'd be able to keep straight for him, and set her loose to figure out the computer program that he'd barely known how to use at a primary level. Yeah, the older gentleman needed help.

The program wasn't that hard, but it'd take some time to

become proficient with it. And she also needed to learn the adventures made available to guests while staying at the lodge. Probably experience them for herself. So much to do, such a steep learning curve.

"I wanted to get acquainted with the space and tasks as soon as possible. All the better on a slow snowy day, since I suspect once the roads clear, it will be the opposite of slow around here."

"Smart." He echoed her earlier response, punctuating it with a wink.

Was he...flirting? Surely not. *Heartbroken* didn't flirt, did it? He'd only just witnessed the matrimonial covenant between his best friend and, apparently, lifelong secret love. Working through the pain set aside, surely a man did not recover from such a blow overnight. If he did...

If he did, it wouldn't speak very highly about the consistency of his nature, would it?

As if that mattered. Well, it did if Lauren was looking for a man. She wasn't, as a matter of fact.

Matt leaned against his elbow, his presence easing deeper into her workspace. "Care to share?"

"Say again?"

"Care to share?" He reached to gently tap the side of her head.

"Do you know what the term *personal space* means?"

That shadowed face grinned again, and laughter gleamed in his eyes. "I do."

He didn't shift backward. Lauren tried not to read a flirtatious anything into it. Just because a man was charming didn't mean he was flirting. Some people had charming imprinted in their DNA. Ashley, for example. Didn't equal flirting. But wow, her sister knew how to work it.

How had Ashley entered into this discussion? Uh, thought? Matt. She was talking to Matt. Who was charming, and not flirting. And as a matter of fact, Lauren could be charming too.

Maybe.

"I don't think we have the same definition," she said.

"Huh." He sipped his coffee, straightening away from her. "Am

I bothering you?"

Darn. Missed that charming mark, and now he was backpedaling. Ugh. "Would that make your morning?" She aimed for wit—the charming kind—again.

"If I was bothering you?"

A lift of her brows sufficed as her answer.

"No." His expression fell serious. Charm wearing sincerity. And didn't that pair nicely? "That would not make my morning. I would think it was interesting though."

"Interesting? Why?"

"People are different, that's why."

Was he an anthropologist? Psychologist? No. Currently, he was a drifter. And a distraction. An attractive, charming distraction.

Heartbroken, she thought over the soft words that had melted through her mind about him. Currently, *heartbroken* wore on Matthew Murphy about as heavy as that dark-blue flannel he wore quite well. Or perhaps she'd become his distraction...

And we have a winner.

The thing about a distraction was that it, by nature, wasn't permanent. It was a come-and-go as you please, take-without-returning situation. She'd walked away from a set of relationships where, though not the same as this setup forming before her, she'd felt used and overlooked. Actually, she'd flown—literally—across the country in an attempt to escape the wearing sense of being unappreciatively used. Did she really want to start off her new life by stepping into another type of the same thing? Being somebody's pawn, so easily put away when the need for her wasn't paramount?

"I had a thought." Matt slid a step backward, and the nonchalance of his earlier countenance slipped a little more. Goodness, that flannel shirt hung on him well, making him appear all rugged and handsome.

Heartbroken, Lauren. And apparently looking for a distraction. Good reasons to establish some kind of guard. A strong kind, to be specific.

Wanting to ignore the attractive build of shoulders, padded

with muscles she assumed he'd gained from working with his dad, and the way his direct gaze seemed to cradle her, she tipped a sassy expression upward and crossed her arms. "Did it hurt?"

Undeterred, he shook his head. "Not as much as other things."

Oh. There it was. *Heartbroken.* A nab of rebuke pinched against her attempt at deflection.

"I wanted to run it by you," Matt said, still on track despite her mental derailment.

"Me?"

"Yes, you."

"Why?"

"To see what you think." He cleared his throat. "I...don't want to freak you out."

"That sounds ominous."

He cleared his throat again. "I thought I'd ask Appleton for a job."

Her lips sealed, and she blinked. "As in, you'd be working here?"

"That's it."

She pointed to the stairway that led to the employees' quarters. "And living here?"

"Right." Watching her, he took another sip, then set the cup on the counter. "You're freaked out."

She stared at him.

"I don't have to," he said.

"Why?" She shook her head, trying to shake off the sudden and powerful sensation that she was in the middle of a mild earthquake and she wasn't entirely sure if she should run or clutch on to something for stability. Like...him.

That was ridiculous.

"Seems like a better choice than Miami." He folded his arms and then shrugged. "You know, financially. A job. Not living in a hotel—well, at least not one that's charging me daily. All those hotheaded bad decisions. Also, I wouldn't be across the continent from my family. And the lodge and resort are sort of awesome. Plus"—he ducked his head, momentarily hiding his eyes, and then looked at her again—"here's the part where you're not supposed to freak out...you're here, so that's a bonus."

"Me?" She squeaked. *Dis.trac.tion. You have been abundantly warned.*

"Yeah. You. It's nice to know someone, don't you think? Have a friend. Maybe one that's not going to let me sulk, be mad at God, get all depressed. You know, bad stuff. I feel like I'm starting over. It would be good to have a familiar face to do it with."

That internal earthquake ended with a jolt that slapped reality hard against her silly emotions. So. She was to be his safe landing.

Not as bad as a distraction.

"Thought maybe you'd like a friend too." He bent, bracing both elbows on the counter and once again squished his oversized frame into the neutral zone between them. "You know, since you left your home and family. Came here all alone. Maybe we'd be good for each other?"

"Yeah..." The word left her mouth a little bit breathy. Which might have come across a lot a bit wrong. She pulled her posture straight. "But I thought about my departure. Long and hard. I didn't just buy a ticket on the first flight to who knows where."

Well, that wasn't nice.

His expression darkened. "I see." Shoulders tightened. "You're good on your own."

She looked to her hand, her fingers twirling a pen. "I'm sorry. That was harsh."

"Hmm. It's true. So." He pushed away from the counter, hands falling to his sides. "I'll take that as a *no*." Turning, he stepped away.

The curve of those well-formed shoulders, and the clench of his fist as he moved toward the exit, provoked a hot cocktail of guilt and pity. Not to mention an internal screaming that flooded her mind with a *No, don't let him leave!*

"Matt." She moved around the counter.

He stopped.

"We're friends?" she asked, the implication of the word *friends* defined by her tone.

He turned, locked a look on her that seemed both vulnerable and confident—and how the heck did that work?

"Could be," he said, the words a soothing offer.

"You won't, um...run me over?"

The crease in his brow made her wish the question back. What must he think?

"I wouldn't dream of it."

She edged toward him. "And friends means..." She left the question hanging.

"Friends." He slid one stride forward.

A smile toyed with her lips. Honestly, a friend sounded nice. Someone dependable who wouldn't take the best of what she could offer and leave nothing but a sense of displacement as a return. Matt could be that sort of friend, right?

Couldn't hurt that he was ruggedly good looking. Not much. Ugh. She wanted to slap the silly out of her mind.

She lifted a finger. "One condition."

He chuckled. "Just one?"

Folding her arms, she tipped her head, searching again for sassy charm, though she had yet to pull it off effectively that morning. Maybe she should give up on that—it'd been Ashley's platform, after all. Not hers.

"You'll never bring up the tux."

"What tux?" The mischievous boy reentered his expression, and he anchored his hands on his hips. "Oh." He snapped, then pointed. "The tux you ruined when you puked on a total stranger in the men's bathroom? That tux?"

She leveled him with the most serious warning look she could muster against the laugh wanting to break free. "Last chance, Murphy."

"Can't make that promise, Matlock." Shaking his head, he took another stride in her direction. As quickly as his mouth had formed a smirk, his expression slipped back into sincerity. "But I can promise you that I do mean friends."

Chapter Six
(in which Matt gains employment)

The fire crackled cheerfully in the big stone fireplace as Matt descended the wide staircase to the front room. A sense of purpose and accomplishment solidified deep within—a feeling he hadn't enjoyed in quite a while. That fire blazing down there in the big open space had been his work, the stacked pine and oak ready to feed the flames also because of him. The walks out front and around the immediate area of Lake Shore's property had been cleared by his sweat and muscles. In spite of a mostly sleepless night, one spent pouring out disappointment and confusion to God, it'd been a good morning.

Smells of savory chicken and fresh-baked rolls drifted from the kitchen, which hid behind the expansive log wall paralleling the wide-open staircase. Matt's stomach rumbled as he set his stride that way. He'd met Mr. Appleton's cook, Emma Lingle, an hour before—shortly after he'd had a productive conversation with the older gentleman. Yes, there was a job for him at Lake Shore Lodge. And Harold Appleton was glad to take him on.

A whisper of *hallelujah* rose from his heart. Though this U-turn in his life hadn't been something Matt had wanted, at least there was sunshine on his horizon. Not to mention warm chicken noodle soup and home-baked bread in his immediate future.

"Ready for lunch?" He paused a few steps away from the front desk, where Lauren worked, remembering her earlier comment about personal space and her sincere question about him running her over—an interesting query in response to his offer of friendship. What had she left behind back east that she would feel the need to define her space? Men? Had there been a romance that had gone south in her past? Or did it all have to do with this Ashley person Lauren hadn't wanted to talk about?

As the questions turned, he wondered about Lauren's night—if it had been restful. Or if she too had done some wrestling with heaven. He wasn't sure why these things about her mattered to the extent they did, but he wanted answers just the same.

Maybe she would tell him. Eventually. He hoped so. Because he was serious about that friendship deal. There was something about her—maybe her chattiness, or the ease he felt around her—he wasn't quite sure. But he did know that a friendship with Lauren Matlock was something of a divine directive. Or perhaps a divine gift.

"Sure, lunch sounds good." She clicked the screen she'd been reading and slipped off a pair of trendy glasses. "Smells awesome, doesn't it?"

Patting his stomach, which gave another begging rumble, Matt nodded.

Lauren laughed. "You worked up an appetite."

"Felt good. You'll have to get out there this afternoon. The air is still chilly, but the sun is warm." He waited for her to pass in front of him and then stepped beside her.

"I planned on it. Mr. Appleton promised a tour of the property."

"Me too," he said.

"So you made it happen?"

He glanced down at her. "The job?"

She nodded.

"Appleton took me on." A swirl of hesitancy settled in his chest. Maybe Lauren hadn't really wanted the job to work out for him? Why that felt important, Matt couldn't say. "That still okay with you?"

Her smile, aimed up at him and strong enough to light her eyes, make the anxious space settle. "I'm glad, Matt. You were right—it'll be good to start this new adventure with a friend."

The hallway elbowed left and led them directly to the kitchen. They passed a door on the right, which Appleton had pointed to when he'd shown Matt around the large main house. "That's me. You're welcome anytime," he'd said. Made Matt feel more like a welcomed grandson than a new employee, and that wasn't a bad thing.

The only part of the morning that had been near to uncomfortable—aside from Matt's initial chat with Lauren—had been the stern look the older gentleman had settled on him during the first part of their interview. "What's your aim with that lovely young woman, Mr. Murphy?"

Obviously he'd meant Lauren, and a sickish sensation of being caught doing something wrong had moved in Matt's gut—which didn't make sense. He hadn't done anything wrong and didn't intend to do anything wrong.

"She's a friend," he'd said.

Other than a miniscule movement on his brow, Mr. Appleton hadn't moved. Just kept a steady gaze locked on Matt. "Your parents are good people, Matt, and I trust them to have raised an honorable son."

"I try to be, sir."

"Good."

There it had ended, a clear implication left between them. *Don't mess with Lauren.* While that moment had been uncomfortable, and Matt didn't particularly enjoy having his character called into question—even mildly—the brief discussion left a lasting impression of security for his new friend. For her sake, Matt was glad Appleton was that sort of man. Though clearly independent, Lauren seemed to need a place to find her footing and safe people to do it around.

"Ah, two fresh faces." Emma Lingle looked over her shoulder as the pair passed from the hallway into her domain, then she turned back to the oven. "The Lord has been good!"

At his side, Lauren hummed. "I could get used to this."

"What's that?" Matt asked.

She stopped in front of the large high counter where several stools stood neatly lined, waiting for use. "The praise toward heaven, accompanied by a promise of food."

Emma set a pan of rolls onto the counter and then waved to a window over a large sink on the far wall. "Don't forget the view."

"No," Matt said. "Definitely don't forget the view."

Lauren slipped onto a stool across from Emma. "I can't wait to get out there, to see all there is to see."

"You'll have to wander the walking path one of these mornings. After the mud clears a bit, of course. But for sure in the morning, when the dew is a million diamonds in the sugar pines and a mist dances on the breeze. The air is a crisp breath of trees and water—fresh and untainted, and the break of new day is a promise waiting to be unwrapped." She tipped her head back, closed her eyes, and inhaled, as if she were standing in the middle of that moment she'd just painted. "Hmmm. It's the best part of the day."

"Sounds like magic."

Emma looked back, smiled, then her attention moved from Lauren to the doorway behind them. "Harold, didn't we pray for help?"

"We did." Appleton's gravelly voice seemed cheerful despite age and wear. "And the Lord has answered."

"It's bound to be a better season."

Matt turned, pulling out a stool as he moved, and motioning for Appleton to take the place, wondering what the last season had been like. Not great, by Emma's comment.

The hand that clapped his shoulder, though gnarled with the hard evidence of arthritis, wore undeniable proof of a life of hard work. Strength still resided in those stiff fingers, just as purpose still shone from the aged face to whom they belonged. Matt knew a sense of kinship. Appleton clearly worked and would continue to work as long as his body would allow.

Determination gripped Matt's mind. This lodge had been

Harold's work—his gift to his wife, and his passion. Matt knew only the resolve to honor that legacy with his own hard work. What had been an initial hope for a new start for himself became, in that moment, something greater. No longer would his aim entirely be about himself and his life's disappointments.

Stand in the presence of the aged. Show respect.

His father's instructions since boyhood surfaced easily in his mind. The directions came from Leviticus, Dad had told him, and honoring the aged was tied intimately with honoring God. Honoring their presence, their life, their work, and their legacy. All of it mattered to the creator of life and time.

Matt waited until Mr. Appleton settled into his chair, and then walked around the work island to stand beside Emma. "What can I do?"

"Eat." She sent him a matter-of-fact nod and then looked back at Mr. Appleton. "After Harold prays, of course."

They bowed, and while that rich, raspy voice lifted thanksgiving for food and for new beginnings, Matt silently lifted his own heart toward the King of heaven. A prayer of his own thanks, and also of curiosity.

Was this Your plan all along?

A chilled current of bitterness intruded into that prayer, one he hadn't invited but one that seemed stubbornly determined to make itself known. Identifying the source wasn't hard. Katrine had been embedded deep, and one day's work in the woods wasn't going to pry her loose so readily. Neither would a new friendship, as promising as it seemed. Nor a new job that suited him so much better than office work and life in the city had.

There was something more there. An edge of...

Conviction?

Over what? Like he'd thought earlier, during his chat with Appleton, he hadn't done anything wrong. Not with Lauren—who had been the topic of interest in that space—and not with Katrine. In fact he'd been particularly careful to do everything right, willing to do whatever it took, whatever she wanted, to make his heart's desire a reality.

Hadn't mattered.

Why would he suffer this distinct arrow of conviction because of that? Hardly seemed fair that God would add insult to injury.

***

The evergreens towered around the lodge, creating a picturesque backdrop to this dreamy adventure that she'd begun. Lauren inhaled deeply as she stopped on the cleanly scooped sidewalk several yards away from the log building where she now lived. The bright steel-blue sky made an impossibly beautiful backdrop for the snow-dusted forest and the silvery waters of the lake that extended beyond and below the front drive. There was both peace and strength in this beauty, a calm that she'd felt missing in her hectic life back home. Something she had secretly longed for since she was a girl. And now there she was, standing in the middle of that brochure she'd pored over for months.

A dream come to life—and she hadn't even wished upon a star.

Thank You. She closed her eyes and felt the praise rise from the depth of her being.

"Is it what you hoped?" Matt stopped beside her—but not *right* beside her. Apparently he was respecting that personal space thing they'd talked about earlier. She still worried over what he thought about that part of their conversation.

Lowering her skyward-turned face, and sweeping her gaze over the scene before her, she smiled. The lodge stood snug within pines, the rough-hewn logs a complement to the setting. A dozen guest rooms resided on the upper floor of the two-story building, all spacious and with an en suite bathroom. Each with a view of the forest on the backside of the property or the lake sprawling downslope out front. Her tiny quarters, complete with a kitchenette, small bedroom, bathroom, and modest sitting area, had been part of an addition built off the back corner of the lodge, not visible from the front. There were two other staff apartments there, both unoccupied until that day. Matt would be moving into one of them by nightfall.

"It's certainly beautiful. Anyone would want to visit, I think."

"Let's hope many do," he said.

Looking back at him, she found his attention on Mr. Appleton as their boss hobbled down the front steps, his aim for them, as he'd promised a tour of Lake Shore's property. There was something uniquely dignified and compassionate about Matt—the way he addressed and behaved toward both Mr. Appleton and Emma Lingle had been entirely respectful. Something that seemed to have been missing from most of her peers, and many of her parents' generation. Though attractive in face and form, and quick with the witty banter, making him fun to be around, that glimpse of deep-seated character swiftly became her favorite thing about Matthew Murphy.

Matt Murphy. The ornery girl within giggled silently at her mental use of his disapproved name. Something to employ on him later perhaps—if their banter so required.

"Sounds like maybe things have been a struggle around here, doesn't it?" Keeping to the more serious topic at hand, Lauren kept her tone low, not wanting the words to carry back to Mr. Appleton.

"That's what I gathered from Emma. Maybe we can do something about that." Mr. Appleton shuffled toward them, and Matt turned around to move toward his side, lifting his voice. "I saw a four-wheeler in the machine shed earlier when I was looking for the snowblower," he called. "I'd be happy to go start it up for you and bring it this way, if you'd like?"

Ah...more evidence. Matt could be the kind of person who could only make her want to be a better person herself. The best sort of friend.

Mr. Appleton swatted the air, as if to brush away the idea. "A walk will do these old bones good. But I do appreciate the thought. Now if you two will quit dawdling along"—a cheeky smirk lifted Mr. Appleton's mouth—"we can finally get to see this place you both now call home."

"Right." Lauren stood at attention. "I'm on my best behavior now. Unfortunately, you'll have to keep a close watch on that guy." She pointed at Matt. "He's been trouble since the moment we met."

A garbled laugh wheezed from Mr. Appleton. "I'd believe that."

"Ha!" Matt elbowed her. "How about we go over again *how* we met. Then he can decide which of us is trouble."

Yikes. Stumbled straight into that. Not that Mr. Appleton didn't already know. Even so, a quick change in subjects might be in order. "How far does the Lake Shore Lodge property go?"

Mr. Appleton stood taller as he scanned the forest, buildings, and then the lake, pride evident in his posture. "Can't see the boundary from here. In fact, to reach the northern line, I would need that four-wheeler. I'll let you find it on your own some other time. If you take the walking trail just past the gazebo"—he motioned to the structure nestled in a stand of trees whose remaining leaves held an orange hue, determined to extend fall against a backdrop of snow-covered pines—"you'll find the boundary marked about a half mile in."

"Who's your neighbor that way?" Matt asked as the trio began toward the gazebo—likely the very one he'd helped build with his dad several years back.

"The government. We're nestled up to the Bureau of Land Management. The trail continues past my property and winds through several acres of protected lands. It's used all year long. Walking, jogging, horseback riding, and cross-country skiing. But you can't take the four-wheeler past our property line. No motorized vehicles."

Matt nodded. "Got it."

They neared a smaller garage-sized building—likely the machine shed Matt had mentioned—sided with logs to match the main lodge. "Are all those activities part of the lodge's draw?"

"Sure are." A glint of mischief tinged Appleton's voice. "And Matt here has inherited all of the responsibility for seeing them done. I'll show you how to hitch the horses later this afternoon, but it'll take several times before you'll be good at it. And more before I trust you to drive a sleigh on your own."

"Sounds good," Matt said. "In the meantime, I'll go through the ski equipment tomorrow. Check the bindings, make sure there are boots that fit each pair of skis." He leaned around Mr. Appleton, who now walked between them, to address Lauren. "Ever been?"

"Skiing? Yes, we have skiing in New England."

"I know that. I meant *cross-country* skiing." He emphasized the difference.

"Uh. No? Is there a difference?"

He chuckled. "Big difference. We'll go. How about snowshoeing?"

She shrugged her shoulders and shook her head in a sort of *sorry to disappoint you* response.

"We'll fix that too." Matt clapped her shoulder. "You'll love it."

Well, she had determined that she needed to experience all that the lodge had to offer. However, the glint in Matt's eyes had her on guard. Honorable though he may be, there was definitely a remnant of little-boy-full-of-trouble in that grown man.

The cleared walk had brought them to the steps of the large gazebo. Though fashioned of rough-hewn logs, complementing the other structures on the property, the craftsmanship in the details gave the rustic material a soft elegance. Mr. Appleton stepped up one of the two risers and placed a hand on a fat pillar. "You remember this, right, Matt?"

"I do." Matt climbed both steps and wandered into the middle, where a stone ring served as a fire pit. "Took Dad and us boys more than a week to finish. It was a fun project. Dad still talks about how much he liked doing it."

A faraway mist clouded Mr. Appleton's expression, something of love and longing, of joy and ache. "It was for our thirtieth. My Essie loved this place, loved the outdoors, and when I showed her the plans for this, she cried. Happy tears." A single laugh lifted from his mouth. "Wasn't always good at finding the right gifts." He pinned a look onto Matt, as if a warning. "Don't give a vacuum to a woman on your anniversary, son. It won't end well."

Matt nodded, chuckling under his breath. "Noted."

"But this"—Mr. Appleton looked over the gazebo—"*this* she loved."

A gentle pause extended as the sacred memory settled—almost as a passing of a gift. A strange thought, and Lauren lingered on it. Why would Mr. Appleton give such a treasured memory to two disconnected strangers?

Likely, it wasn't that at all. She'd just been swept up in the romance of it all.

Not here for romance, Lauren. Neither is Matt Murphy.

She refused to look at Matt and determined to keep that truth clutched front and center. She'd come to find her independence, and Matt was heartbroken. Both more than enough reason for her to stay sensible.

At Mr. Appleton's beckon, they moved on. Keeping to his slower pace, they wound through the immediate features of the lodge. Lauren peeked in the machine shed, finding the four-wheeler Matt had mentioned, the snowblower he'd used earlier that morning, a wall full of narrow skis and poles, shelves of low-top boots, and on the other side of the shelves, several aluminum snowshoes—what she assumed were snowshoes—hung neatly. In the middle of the large shed, a beautiful sleigh waited for winter's full glory, the seats that would accommodate four to six people, including the driver, covered carefully by a protective canvas tarp.

Oh, the adventures that awaited! A thrill raced through her body. Guilt for leaving her family—particularly her sister—notwithstanding, moving to the Lake Shore Lodge might have been the best decision of her whole life.

Past the machine shed was a small barn and wood-railed corral housing two horses. Though not tall like the Belgians she'd seen at a parade several years back, both had the stocky build of a draft breed. Lauren made a note to look up small draft horses and hoped she could participate in their care. After the corral, they found the mouth of the trail. Wide enough to accommodate the sleigh, beneath the slushy snow, the dirt pack gave evidence of frequent use. She'd explore it tomorrow—in the morning just as Emma had suggested.

"This is as far as I go these days," Mr. Appleton said. For a long moment, he looked down the narrow lane that curved into the mixed forest, the longing to visit past this boundary obvious. "You two will have to see what's beyond on your own. Don't test the lake waters this time of year. In the summer, we'll get out the paddleboards and kayaks that are stored in the attic of the machine shed. But I don't mess with them past September. I'm not interested in flirting with hypothermia."

"Got it." Matt turned back toward the lodge and scanned the property from that vantage point.

Lauren followed his lead, loving the view. Behind the tree line at the back of the lodge, up a small hill and barely visible, two smaller structures winked between the swaying branches. She pointed. "What are those?"

Both men focused on the place of her interest. Mr. Appleton hesitated, then moved back down the path they'd come. "The original house and cabin. They're closed now."

"Closed?" The question slipped out before she processed the distance in Mr. Appleton's response.

"Yes. Closed. Haven't used them in several years."

"Oh."

"I could go check them." Matt fell into step beside Mr. Appleton. "See what it might take to make them useable again?"

Lauren caught up, glancing at Mr. Appleton as she realized the hesitation in her boss's voice wasn't simply because the cabin and house had apparently fallen into disrepair. She'd overstepped, she was sure. And now Matt was too.

"No." After several steps made in an uncomfortable quiet, Mr. Appleton shook his head, his answer equally determined and regretful. "No, I think not yet."

Chapter Seven
(in which Matt loses his temper)

Mist swirled toward the treetops, softly cloaking the pines like a bride's veil. Emma had been right—this morning walk through the forest proved to be enchanted, and for over a week now, Lauren had slipped her feet into her insulated boots and made a solitary journey down the path and into the public lands. She hadn't pushed much more than two miles in, though Mr. Appleton said that the trail would loop back if she continued on it, the total distance varying between five and twelve miles, depending on which loop she took. New to wandering woods on her own, she hadn't pressed herself yet.

Prayer came easily as her boots trailed over leaves and mud, taking her deeper into the enchantment and easing away the cares she might have for the upcoming day. Even with the distant buzz of a chainsaw where Matt was working already, Lauren basked in a peace that she'd thirsted for. Her biggest worries had lessened as her first week slipped by. The program Mr. Appleton had purchased for the lodge quickly became familiar to her, and taking reservations, planning small gatherings, and organizing events were her strong suit.

This job fit perfectly, and this setting filled her with gratitude. *Thank You for new opportunities. And new friends. For Mr. Appleton—such a deeply caring man.* The tie between herself and her employer developed quickly into something more familial than economical, and she would guess that had always been the case with every employee Mr. Appleton had had. She could see the same strengthening relationship forming between Matt and their employer too. And Emma clearly had a loyal bond as well. Mr. Appleton shepherded them with care, and while he obviously loved his lodge and took pride in the work he'd put into this place, he loved his people better. Begged the question—*what if we all valued others in such a way?*

"Thank You for his example," Lauren prayed—the words now an audible whisper, spoken as if God Himself walked these woods at her side. "And for Matt. Thank You for his friendship, and his example too."

She paused there, casting her thoughts over the man who had rescued her at the airport. On the surface, he was lighthearted. Witty—loved to banter with her, and that was fun. Maybe even was a borderline flirt. But Matthew Murphy possessed many layers, depths that made him both complex and endearing. In reality, she didn't see him much during the day. He worked outside, and by the amount of food he consumed and the dirt and sweat he ended his days wearing, she was certain he worked hard.

Between sorting the winter equipment—which apparently had become a tedious job demanding several days' attention—cutting and then splitting diseased trees for firewood, and general everyday maintenance around the lodge, the man labored ten to twelve hours a day. And he seemed to thrive in it.

Then there was his faith. Though it was something he could have simply used as a ploy when the need called for it—as she'd suspected back at the airport—Matthew Murphy wasn't the sort. His prayers, unashamedly lifted when given the opportunity, were deep and heartfelt. In the mornings, she found him sitting in a leather armchair near the fire he'd built to drive away the chill, reading his Bible. And he'd asked her for the reference for the verse she'd told him about at the airport—the one about God not forgetting His people—because he wanted to read it in context and commit it to memory. Wispy believers didn't do things like that. Matt's faith wore boots and walked daily.

Beneath all of that, there was a lingering...something. Lauren suspected it was that heartbreak thing. He kept it in check. Didn't wallow in the disappointment. But there were moments, like when he prayed after his morning reading. His head bowed, he'd silently go before God, and often his quiet moments before the throne would end with his shoulders bent, face in his hands. When he stood, though she felt ashamed that she watched—intruding on something so personal and not her business—Lauren couldn't help but see traces of painful submission etched into that handsome face. As if *not my will* had carved beneath his skin and he was fighting to hold on to that surrender.

Ease his heartache, Father. Give him strength to fight for this surrender, and faith to know You work for good in the lives of Your people.

She reached her turnaround point on the trail as her prayer for Matt ended, and as she switched directions, her thoughts changed too.

Ashley hadn't given up. Shouldn't surprise her. Lauren knew her sister to have the determination of a lioness on the hunt. Not necessarily a bad thing, but for Lauren, her sister's unswayable nature had become exhausting. One of many reasons Lauren had felt the need to leave.

Their text conversation the night before had been yet another example.

Anderson mixed up two of my meetings this week. Lauren, this isn't going to work.

Hi to you too, sis. My week has been good, thank you for asking.

Face to face, Lauren wouldn't have dared that kind of response. Snark was so much easier via text. Wasn't sure if that was a good thing or a bad thing.

Sorry. But I'm in a real situation here. I can't have incompetence right now.

I'm sorry Anderson mixed up some things. He'll get it—it's only been a week since he started. Give him some grace.

I can't afford that.

Not sure you have a choice. Unless you can find someone to take his place who can handle your crazy, always switching, always shoving more into it schedule.

I had someone. She ditched me.
Please don't go there again. This is my life, my choice.
Why now, Lauren? I really need you.

Lauren had dropped back onto her bed, wishing that she'd been asleep when Ashley had started this thread. Actually, Ashley should have been asleep. It was past one in the morning back east. No wonder her younger sister had issues with almost everything. Lack of sleep did not pair well with a busy life.

She'd looked back at that last sentence. Ashley had always "really needed" something. Her freshman year in high school, Lauren's junior year, Ashley had "really needed" the prom dress Lauren had picked out and saved for. Lauren's senior year, Ashley "really needed" to go on the youth group ski trip that had generally been reserved for those soon graduating. Sophomore year in college, Ashley "really needed" Lauren to spend two nights a week tutoring her in accounting because she couldn't possibly be seen going to the intervention study group the teacher had made available.

Her sister often "really needed" insignificant things too. Lauren's car for a weekend. A quick loan. To borrow Lauren's new wool coat...

Small things. Minor incidents that shouldn't have mattered. But they did when they started to add up. And once Ashley had her mind set on the vacating seat in the state house of representatives, she "really needed" Lauren. Not just her vehicle or clothes or ability to run Excel. Ashley demanded *all* of her.

Perhaps Lauren should have felt honored. Being needed was a good thing, wasn't it? Instead, she resented the implication that her life had become only as significant as far as it was disposable to Ashley. And Ashley never saw it. Never understood—or cared to try to understand.

Which had been the final bitter drop. One that still tasted acrid in Lauren's mouth. And not one she'd yet been willing to lift heavenward.

***

Thanks for everything. Nothing like a best friend to ruin your life.

The text had been branded in Matt's mind. Almost two weeks post-event, and suddenly John sent two sentences before blocking Matt's number. At least, Matt assumed he'd been blocked, since the responses he'd sent since receiving that cryptic message were still not marked as delivered.

Didn't know what to do about that. He wanted to defend himself—at least he hadn't tried to stop the wedding. Hadn't tried to talk Katrine out of the marriage, even when given the clear opportunity to do so. Leaving before the ceremony began had seemed like the best thing to do, and up until last night, he would have stood firmly on that claim.

Until, following John's text by only an hour, a message from Katrine came through.

I couldn't do it.

Clarity. John and Katrine were not married.

A message that should have unlocked all his resentment, allowing relief to flow freely where there'd been frustration, instead amplified confusion and guilt.

What had he done?

Matt wasn't sure how to process the news or how he should respond to Katrine's text. So he didn't. Thought long and hard about deleting both messages, though ultimately he didn't do that either. It'd been a long night. Despite limited sleep, he had more than enough anxious energy to fuel his day. He'd risen before daybreak, built a fire, read his Bible, and then plowed into work.

The project with the skis was nearly completed, and he needed something more physically demanding to spill the excessive energy into, so he found a chainsaw, snatched the hacksaw, and set out for a stand of pines about two hundred yards off the trail. He'd noticed a couple days back the area had shown significant bark beetle damage—a fire danger to the forest and an eyesore for the tourists.

For nearly two hours, he'd cut and sawn, felling one whole tree and trimming damage off several others before focusing on carving firewood out of the downed limbs and trunk. Sawdust littered the area, covering what remained of the snow, and likely him—from stocking cap to boots. Still, those texts stayed fresh in his mind, as well as the heavy guilt that had turned in his gut.

No part of it seemed fair, and rather than working out his frustration, cutting firewood had only amped him up more. With a grip on a three-foot section of trunk he'd set up on a makeshift sawhorse, he lifted the bulk of the log and hurled it into a pile of cut wood waiting to be stacked. The impact snapped thinner logs, sending a loud cracking through the otherwise quiet of the trees.

"Why?" he hollered against the serene forest.

No answer. Not that he'd expected one.

The apex of his temper spent, Matt lowered onto a stump. Slumping forward, he caught his head in his hand and gripped his hat. "Help me with this," he whispered.

A soft gust moved through the boughs, its gentle whisper joining the sporadic chatter of birds. Matt wanted to sink into their world—apart from complicated relationships and life's massive gullies. He could be a woodsman, a survivalist out in nature all on his own. No one to bother him, to muck up his heart and mind. Seemed like an ideal escape—

A branch snapped in the distance, somewhere toward the trail, and the conversation of the birds silenced.

"Matt?" Her voice. And then the crack of another limb.

Ah yes. Then there was Lauren. Uncomplicated, chatty, and good natured. He would miss that friendship, even new as it was, were he to skulk off into the woods. Miss the banter. The way she'd blush at the mention of a tux. The way she bit her bottom lip when she worked, and the *aha* look that would capture her face when she figured out something new with the program she was learning. The way wonder possessed her when she wandered through Lake Shore's breathtaking beauty.

"Matt, are you okay?" The cream of her coat peeked through a clump of three trees as she pushed her way through the mingling branches.

"Over here, Lauren." He stood, made an attempt to brush off the million shavings of chewed-up pine covering his arms and chest, and then stepped toward the boughs trying to hold her captive.

She emerged, green needles speckled on her white coat and hat. Brushing at them, she picked her way over downed limbs toward him. "Hey. I was worried. Thought I heard you."

Heat brushed his face. "Yeah. Sorry. I was..."

Mad? Yelling at God? Sure he was alone? Yep, to all of those.

Lauren's concerned expression softened, and as she passed by, she squeezed his arm and then continued toward the pile of firewood lying helter-skelter on the forest floor.

"Looks like you've been productive," she said.

"I..." Sheesh. He couldn't even form a sentence.

With her glance, he saw both compassion and understanding. Also things he'd miss about her.

"I was just out walking." She turned back to the mess and began organizing the logs. Length had been the same—he'd cut them that way on purpose. Lauren picked through the jumbled pile, finding the narrower pieces. "Praying too. I was actually just praying for you."

His chest tightened. Attempting to ignore the discomfort, he joined her efforts, only his focus turned to the biggest of the pieces. They sorted in comfortable, quiet companionship, though Matt wondered what Lauren was thinking. Had she figured that his outburst had been out of anger? Could she guess the source of his frustrations?

She didn't press, and that made sharing with her seem somehow both important and safe.

"I heard from Katrine last night." He began a second row on one end of a four-foot section of similar-sized logs, making sure the new row settled into the cradle made by two logs fitted together below. He'd leave the stack, once they had it organized, so that it could season over the next year. Then the jackets would need removed, the logs split. Enough work to keep him busy and employed there at the lodge. A place Katrine would never occupy.

"Wow." Lauren glanced at him but kept working. "Been a couple weeks, right? You didn't hear from her sooner?"

"No. Didn't expect to." Especially since he'd assumed she'd gone to Hawaii with John on their honeymoon. He stood straight, attention lost somewhere near the treetops. "She didn't go through with it." The words were cast toward the sky in a mix of disbelief and confusion.

It took several moments before Matt realized Lauren had stilled. When reality sank back into his awareness, he looked back at her, finding an expression of pity and worry that made him feel less like a man and more like a teenage kid.

Also, a little defensive—thanks to John's text, mostly. "I didn't try to talk her out of it."

She set the two logs in her hand onto the growing neat pile. "Didn't think that you had."

"Well, you're the only one then."

"What does that mean?"

"John texted me last night too."

Her eyes grew wide. "Yikes?"

"Yeah, yikes. Two quick shots of accusation, and then he blocked me. He thinks it's my fault—that I've ruined his life."

Her lips pressed as she stood there studying him. Not knowing her reaction—but guessing her thoughts to be the worst sort—pricked at his already frayed nerves. "I swear, Lauren. I didn't do anything. I left—that's all." His tone barked as the muscles in his jaw tensed.

She winced and then responded with something breathy and injured. "I believe you."

Matt shut his eyes, regathering his self-control. Did it matter what Lauren believed? Clearly, yes, it did. Why wouldn't it—who wanted people thinking the worst about them?

"Matt?"

He readjusted his stocking cap, inhaled deeply, and then forced himself to meet her gaze. "I'm sorry, Lauren. I shouldn't dump any of this on you. It's not your fault. Not your mess."

"We're friends, Matt. Remember?" She moved a foot closer. "You can tell me, if you want to. Even if you think I won't approve or if it's something you're embarrassed about. If you need someone to talk it through with, you can tell me, and it'll end there. I promise."

Sincerity had a face in that moment. She had sweet brown eyes and dark thick hair that had a propensity to curl at the ends. Matt stepped around the woodpile he'd been making and stopped in front of Lauren. "That's a bold promise."

"Well." A sweet though mischievous smile lit her eyes. "I did puke on you first. Seems like a fair trade."

The anxiety he'd wrestled all morning unraveled, and the world refocused. Though his life, and the two relationships he'd held most important for more than five years, were now in chaos, as Matt looked on Lauren, those angry tethers loosened.

Thank You for this woman. The lift of gratitude helped to undo some of the irritation with God that had been pestering him all morning.

Lauren reached to squeeze his arm. Her white hat had been peppered with wood shavings and pine needles, and the coat she wore also had become littered, not to mention streaked with black mud. Matt lifted his hand to brush a smattering of needles from her shoulder. "This ski coat is going to get ruined if you keep at this."

Her forehead wrinkled at his change in topics, and then she looked down at her sleeve. "It's just a coat."

"It's a nice one. We shouldn't ruin it." Tipping his face skyward, he studied the gathering clouds overhead. "It's going to get wet again soon, I think. I can work on this by myself—or if you want to help, I shed my outer layer a while ago." He motioned to a tree behind him. "You can use my coat instead."

Lauren tipped her head to one side, bit her bottom lip. "Do you want me to go?"

"No." He didn't need to think on it. "No, I like you here."

"Then I'll stay." She maneuvered her way across the forest floor and gripped his brown work coat. Holding it up, she asked,

"You're sure?"

About wanting her there? Or about the coat? Didn't matter. The answer was the same.

"I'm sure."

Chapter Eight
(in which Matt and Lauren roast marshmallows)

She'd stayed outside longer than she'd planned. But as Lauren changed into warm, dry clothes, her concern focused more on Matt than on the chill that sank bone deep through her limbs, or on the work that she'd need to catch up on at the desk.

While they'd stacked, he'd settled into the easygoing, calmer Matt she'd met two weeks before. But the laughter they'd shared in bits and pieces hadn't really made his eyes dance. Not like they had in previous days. This woman, Katrine, had really done something to him, and Lauren found a surprising amount of resentment edging into her heart toward this person she'd never met.

Help me to think rightly, Lord. Show me kindness and how to be the kind of friend Matt needs.

With a dry teal sweater soft on her shoulders and a fresh pair of dark skinny jeans in place, Lauren replaced her walking boots with a pair of tall riding-style boots and stopped at the mirror to pull back her hair.

Ringlets escaped the hair tie she'd secured at the base of her head, framing her face of their own design—which, in her opinion, was a touch on the wild side. Oh well. She didn't have time to tame her curls with a blow-dryer and brush, and it was only pride that made her hesitate with the thought in the first place. She did have work to do, and taking advantage of Mr.

Appleton's kind spirit as an employer didn't seem right.

She tapped down the stairs from the employees' quarters to the front desk, finding the fire that had been a mere flicker when they'd returned from the woods was now a full blaze. Matt didn't pause for long, that was for sure, and Lauren smiled, appreciating the warmth as she rounded the front desk. On the lower counter, near her computer, a large mug sat, steam drifting a lovely invitation. She inhaled, the rich aroma of a dark mocha teasing her taste buds.

Her favorite.

A scrap of paper had been anchored beneath the warm drink. *Thanks for your help. It's Emma's day off, but she left us a spread. I'll see you at lunch.*

Her belly tickled. Hard working, kind, thoughtful...handsome. How had this Katrine person not fallen for Matthew Murphy?

Oh...danger. *Friends, Lauren. You promised.*

Yes, she had. And she had work to do, anyway. Work that required her full attention, and with a quick glance to the oversized wall clock behind the front desk, she found it was already past ten. That gave her about two hours, give or take, to catch up on what she hadn't been doing while she'd been out stacking firewood. Two hours before that good-looking, generous *friend* would be back for lunch.

She'd best get to it.

As had been her pattern over the past five days, she started with email inquiries. Three new reservations harvested there. She moved on to her prescribed reading—articles pertaining to advertising in the hospitality industry. If she and Matt were going to help this season turn a better profit than the previous year, she needed to learn how to bring in more visitors. The academic in her sent her studying, and while she liked learning, it did take time. Three articles and several notes later, she clicked to a graphics site and worked on an ad copy that she planned to post on social media.

Another glance behind her told her it was ten minutes after noon. Her stomach confirmed the hour, yawning an intrusive complaint. She turned toward the bank of windows that faced the front deck. No Matt.

She had some time to post a few ads and to try the suggested trick she'd read about this morning. In the search bar at the top, she entered in *vacation rentals*.

Wowza. She had a lot of options to dig through. Clicking on the largest group, she scrolled through the posts until she found those with the words *California* or *Lake Tahoe* or *Mountain Retreat*. In the comments, she dropped a link to the website she'd updated last week. Hoping she wasn't wasting her time, she set a goal of a dozen link drops and kept scrolling.

A pounding on the steps preceded the mild squeak of the door, alerting Lauren to Matt's entry as she met her goal. She looked up to find his back to her as he shut the door and wiped his feet.

"Hey." He glanced over his shoulder and then moved toward the fireplace, one arm cradling a stack of wood. "Did you get done with what you needed to do this morning?"

She slipped off her work stool and gripped the now empty mug. "Mostly. I have a few phone calls to make yet. But there'll be time after lunch. You?"

The bundle of logs clanked as he dumped them into the box on the left side of the hearth. "Don't think I'll ever be done. But that's not a bad thing. I like staying busy."

"I can tell."

He brushed at his arms and hands. "Hope I didn't set you back this morning."

"No, I don't think so. First guests won't check in until the day after tomorrow, and even then, only three of the rooms are reserved. Now that I've got the website updated, I've been working on marketing."

"Wow. You are definitely the right girl for this job. Appleton will be pleased." With a quick swipe, Matt removed his stocking cap. The thick stand of his dark hair poked every which way in wild revolt.

Lauren snickered.

"What?" He peered down at her, pretending a scowl. "I give you a compliment, and you laugh at me?"

"You look like a bear who got tangled up with a power cord."

"Huh." He forked his fingers through the mess on his head. "To think I made you a mocha and everything."

"That is true." She lifted the empty mug. "Thanks for that."

"Well, I guess I owed you. Since you stayed out there in the wet and cold to make sure I didn't lose it again."

"That's not why I stayed."

He locked a look on her, appreciation gleaming in those brown eyes. Oh, a girl could read things into those depths...

Better not.

She turned and stepped toward the hallway to the kitchen. "I'm hungry. You?"

"Always."

They found a plate of covered sandwiches with their names taped to the plastic wrap and a jug of apple cider in the fridge. On the counter, also marked with their names, sat a basket with a pair of apples and four sets of s'mores packets—something Emma had been putting together for the hospitality bundles Lauren would be placing in the guest rooms the following day. After heating two mugs of cider, Matt grabbed the plate of sandwiches and Lauren picked up the basket from the counter. She followed him back to the front room, where they set their lunch on the floor in front of the fire, like a picnic.

"Not a bad deal," Matt said after they'd prayed. "Almost like living at home again, only I get paid for the chores I do."

Lauren laughed. "It is nice—although I'm thinking that if I don't watch it, I'll end up gaining weight before spring comes." Such an awkward thing to say to a guy. Lauren wanted to smack her forehead.

Matt shook his head and then shrugged. "I think you'll stay busy enough not to worry about it."

If she'd been fishing for a compliment, she would have probably been disappointed. Good thing she wasn't. She bit into the turkey, cranberry, and almond on a croissant, savoring the tangy-sweet combination. Matt plowed into his lunch as well, eating like he was, in fact, starving.

The dance of the flames and snap of burning wood served as the only sound between them for some time. That didn't change until Matt dusted off his fingers and downed the last of his cider.

"Why would Katrine contact me now, after two weeks, do you think?" He shifted to his knees, opening one of the s'mores packets and then reaching for a fire fork that resided in a metal tin on the right side of the hearth.

From her seat opposite, Lauren couldn't see his expression. "I don't know. Seemed strange to me too. Also, that you hadn't heard something sooner from John—and that both texted you the same night."

His profile angled to her, giving her a view of his clamped jaw and furrowed brow. Once again, a flash of resentment ignited within, aimed straight at Katrine. Why would a woman torture a man like that?

"What did she say?" Lauren couldn't resist asking.

"Just that she didn't go through with it."

Sure that she scowled, Lauren dipped her face down, fiddling with a s'mores packet as a cover-up while she worked to conceal the ugly feelings stirring inside. Matt must have had a reason he kept an emotional hold on a woman who hadn't wanted him.

"We'd been friends for a long time. Since high school."

Surprised by the quiet opening of his heart, Lauren glanced up. He stared at the dancing flames, roasting a mallow.

"I met John in college, and he came home with me one weekend. That's how he and Katrine met. He didn't know that I'd had a secret crush on her for a couple of years, and when they started dating, I just tried to bury everything about it." He glanced at her but didn't meet her eyes. "I don't know—maybe I shouldn't have, but I didn't want to be that guy, you know? The one who moved in on his friend's girlfriend. So..."

"Yeah, I get it. But..."

"Thing was, they broke up. Several times, actually—over the course of about five years. Every time they did, John would be angry and devastated, and Katrine would—"

He didn't finish, and for several heartbeats, silence drew out. Lauren was left to fill in the blanks.

"She turned to you?"

"Yeah. I guess." Again, his fingers plowed through his hair, making the thick mess stand on end.

"But you never told her how you felt?"

"No. Not out loud." When he looked at her, where she'd guessed there would be regret, there instead flared a fire of betrayal. "Never seemed quite right—the timing. But since I'm spilling my guts to you here, the truth is, I thought she knew. Every time. How could she not know? I always sided with her. Always did what she wanted—big and small things. Even changed my studies in college to match her ideals for me."

"What did she want for you?"

"A *real* job." His mallow toasted to perfection, he sat back. "Something in an office with a bulky paycheck."

"Doesn't sound like you."

His huffed laugh seemed more of resentment than humor, and with the s'more he'd been fixing ready, he passed it over to her. "You and I have known each other two weeks, and you can see that. She—" His words cut off with a bitter edge.

Lauren prayed for wisdom—and for the building dislike of a woman she didn't know to ebb away. "Why did you hang on to her?"

His lips pressed hard, and anger turned his expression cold.

"I'm sorry," Lauren whispered.

As he took the s'more packet she'd been fiddling with, his countenance lost the glint of anger and returned to confusion. He stabbed the new mallow and reached it toward a hot spot of embers. "My dad asked me that once. Why I held out hope for a woman like her."

What exactly had his dad seen? What had Mr. Murphy meant by a *woman like her*? Not wanting to provoke that hard flash of anger again, Lauren kept the questions silent.

"I don't know." Resignation sagged in his voice, and then he turned a look of utter defeat toward her. "I really don't know,

Lauren."

She had no idea what to say.

***

The phone pressed a chill into his hands as he passed it from palm to palm. His small apartment, lit only with a single lamp near his chair, felt too quiet. Too cold.

Matt had no idea what to do. Nor could he explain why he'd shared with Lauren all that he'd told her.

She must think him such a loser. And wasn't he?

Why would you pursue a woman who thinks of only herself?

His dad's words, spoken in frustration and disappointment at the crest of an argument over two years before, still rang as clearly in his mind as they had on that day. They'd been working on a job Matt had taken a weekend trip home to help with, building a she-shed for a client who had been difficult at best. Demanding. Unreasonable. And, apparently, one who reminded Dad of Katrine. In a lot of ways, Dad had not been wrong.

Katrine had a diva streak. Even back then, Matt hadn't been able to deny that undesirable truth. But there was something about her, something strong and...addictive. Even in his misery then—at the time acting as Katrine's safety net while she and John were at another impasse in their relationship—he'd seen a future that felt possible. One that was happy, one that had him content to bring in the paydirt Katrine seemed to need, and her blissfully satisfied with him at her side. So convinced of that future, he'd told God how perfect it would be, if only God would move...

The sharp edge of conviction sliced against his heart. There. Right there was something he needed to deal with.

The phone still in his hand, now warm, he shifted his attention back to the screen. Unwilling to admit the avoidance that move was, he hit the Home button and reread the text he'd received twenty minutes before.

Matt, are you there? Did you get my text this morning? I really need you to talk to me.

With pain in every squeeze, his heart throbbed. His hands shook. Powerful emotions swirled. Longing. Fear. Frustration.

Shame?

Yes. That was in there too. And he had a vague understanding as to why. This...this Ferris wheel—this unending up and down ride not only he but John and Katrine were on—it needed to stop.

He could stop it.

Just let this go. Change direction and walk away.

If only that was as easy to do as it was to think.

The phone vibrated in his fingers again. Against better counsel, he looked.

Please Matt.

Shoulders rolling in as if crumbling under pressure, Matt tapped the screen.

I'm here. But I'm not sure we have anything to say to each other.

You left the wedding. We need to talk.

You weren't marrying me, Katrine. My not being there shouldn't have stopped you from getting married.

How could you say that? I needed you.

There's something really wrong with that, Katrine.

She didn't respond, and the scroll dots disappeared. Fisting the phone, he pressed it against his forehead.

What if she got it, finally? What if this moment turned into one of those pop hit songs where suddenly she saw what had been in front her all along? Maybe now, she got it. Then... What?

Two weeks ago, that would have been his happy ending.

Son, you're free to make your choices, and I'll always love you. But the thing about our lives is that the choices we make today will play out in all our tomorrows. Make sure what you grip now won't be bondage in your future.

Dad had spoken calmly by then, as they'd loaded the pickup to go home. As irritated as Matt had been with his father that afternoon, and, really, anytime Katrine had come up for quite a while, he knew without a doubt Dad spoke from a place of love, a heart longing for good for his son.

Had Katrine ever been that way for him? Or even for John? Had her heart ever wanted what was best for either of the men she'd entangled? Matt didn't like the emptiness that question left, which made the idea of her finally understanding what he'd wanted from her more than a little terrifying.

A sensation of landing on quicksand suddenly came over him. He set the phone on the table in front of the chair and stood to cross the apartment. An impulse to pull open the door to the hallway and step down to Lauren's entry surged. What would she say?

She'd think he was pathetic. He *was* pathetic. But still, maybe her blunt-but-in-a-kind-way of handling things would loan him the resolve he needed to cut ties, move on.

Was that fair of him? No, likely not. Maybe he should just find his big-boy pants and buckle them on.

Rolling his shoulders back, he studied the night sky beyond the window. *Do You still hear me? I've landed myself somewhere more complicated than it looked. I need help.*

Though the clouds had cleared, leaving a crisp, starry canvas with enough enormous beauty to steal one's breath, Matt fought against the feeling of being unseen. He studied the hand he'd braced against the window frame and then shut his eyes.

Sleep. A man needs sleep to think clearly. Another one of his dad's maxims.

Pushing away from the glass, he padded toward the small bedroom containing a twin bed, a nightstand, and a modest wardrobe, which he'd filled several days before, after receiving the box of clothes he'd asked his brother Connor to pack up from Matt's city apartment and mail. Once his lease was up in December, he'd move the rest of his things out. Hopefully, Connor or Dad and Mom would have space for storage. Or perhaps it was time to get rid of a bunch of stuff and start over.

That idea solidified, easing the sense of being sucked in deeper. Moving on in life. Complicated, yes. But...

His phone buzzed on the table in the front room. Knowing who made the thing jump to life, he told himself to ignore it.

The compulsive side of himself did not comply, and within

thirty seconds he was reading Katrine's latest text.
I think I need you, Matt. Tell me where you are so we can figure this out.

Chapter Nine
(in which Lauren helps with the horses)

"Do you think there are people who can be toxic, even if they don't mean to be?"

Lauren paused her typing, her eyes still on the screen at her desk, but her attention completely derailed. Bad timing on that. She had two groups—rather large ones—who had responded to yesterday's marketing experiment. Both had inquired about activities and availability near Thanksgiving. This was kind of a big breakthrough, and she needed to nail it.

But who could ignore a question like that?

She finished typing the last bit of information—when the lodge would be available to the second group and the total cost for all available rooms—and turned her attention toward Matt. He stood near the fire he'd just stoked, brushing off wood slough that wasn't on his thermal long-sleeve shirt poking out from under his CalTech tee. Vulnerability marked his movements, as did his lack of eye contact. She had no doubt about whom he'd been thinking.

What spell had that woman cast?

"Do I think people can be toxic?"

"Yeah." He stopped moving and slowly lifted his gaze until they met hers. "Even if they don't mean to. You know, like they're not intending to wreck you, but that's just how things play out. Does that happen?"

"Yes, that happens." She hadn't needed a moment to consider, because as much as she didn't understand his attachment to a woman Lauren was having a hard time pulling up any sympathy for, she had a sister who, to a large degree, did the same thing to her. Ashley wasn't evil. She wasn't even necessarily *entirely* selfish. Her sister had some blind spots—and didn't everyone? "Anything in particular you want to talk about?"

He scanned the room and then stopped on the windows to the deck. By the working of his jaw, she guessed he had a lot he needed to talk about. The wanting to part...

Hmm. He had brought it up.

"Matt?"

As if snapped back to the present, he jerked his face back toward her. After a beat of study—a storm simmering in his eyes—the grooves that had carved into his forehead smoothed, and the tightness of his jaw eased. Shoving his hands into his jeans pockets, he padded, sock footed, over to her workspace and then leaned on the countertop of the front desk. "What are you doing right now?"

From heartbroken and tortured to easygoing charm.

Lauren drew a quiet breath, deciding to let it go. "Finishing a letter to a potential guest. They want to come for a family reunion."

"Sounds like a good bite."

"I hope so. We've got to make it a better year for Mr. Appleton, right?"

The corners of his mouth lifted. "He was happy with the website you designed. Nice work on that."

"Thanks." So stalling was his newest technique. Matt was all sorts of interesting.

He leaned against his elbows and peeked over the counter. "You ready for a break yet?"

"I'm not hungry, if that's what you're asking."

"That's weird. How can you not be hungry? We ate lunch, like, two hours ago."

She sighed. "Matt, do you need something?"

His posture slumped casually; the earlier pensive man now untraceable. "Thought you should go outside. The rain stopped. Sun's shining. Maybe you'd like to come fork some hay for the horses with me?"

"Will I get to pet them?"

The corners of his eyes crinkled in victory. "Only if they like you."

With a sassy tip of her chin, she smirked. "As if that would be a problem."

He smacked the counter. "Perfect. Let's go."

While he sauntered toward the door, stopping to slip on his boots and then grabbing hers, Lauren finished her letter and hit Send. Hopefully, her contact would find everything satisfactory. Hopefully, she'd just secured a full lodge for the rest of the month, save Thanksgiving day itself, and Mr. Appleton would be pleased.

She took the pair of mud boots Emma had magically summoned for Lauren's second day on the job and slipped her socked feet into them. "Hey, Matt?"

"Yes, Lauren?" His hand rested on the door handle, ready to open it once she secured her footwear.

"I hope I'm not toxic to you."

The serious version of the man settled a look on her. "Never."

He unlatched the door and made his way outside. Lauren followed, praying his proclamation would prove true. For them both.

***

"I told you, liking me wouldn't be a problem." With alfalfa flakes dusting her cream stocking hat, Lauren flashed a grin toward Matt as Bucky nuzzled her arm.

Matt grinned. No, liking Lauren was about as likely to be a problem for anyone as a ninety-five-degree day was in their immediate future. Matt shoved the pitchfork into the grass bale he'd been dividing and moved toward the happy pair at the smaller feed bunk.

"Clearly he's found the love of his life," he said wryly. "But I wouldn't let it go to your head, since you're wearing a good amount of his favorite treat." Ungloving his hand, he reached to brush the small green flakes off her head and then her shoulders.

"Are you saying he's only nice to me because of the food?"

"Well, there's that, and this guy is a back-pocket sort. He'd be in your lap if you had grain and would let him snuggle up there. Pretty sure he thinks he's a puppy."

Lauren curled an arm under the stocky horse's chin. "Don't you listen to him. He's just jealous."

Jealous... interesting. Of Bucky's attention, or Lauren's? Such a thought. His head was a mess, and his heart was in worse shape. *Don't mess with Lauren.* That had been Appleton's implication. Better take it seriously. She had no need to be caught in the emotional pretzel he'd landed himself in.

"There's that look." Lauren dropped the hug she'd held on Bucky and slid a half step closer to Matt. "She text you again?"

"Are you clairvoyant?"

"Definitely not." She pushed her hands into her coat pocket. Bucky sniffed her shoulder and then nudged her elbow. With a laugh, she turned half to the horse and touched his muzzle. She spoke, but her attention stayed on the horse. "You're an easy read, Matt Murphy. Your eyes won't lie."

Couldn't be completely true. Katrine never seemed to understand. Or, maybe she had... The thought provoked a sour burn in his gut.

"*Matthew* Murphy." He stepped around her to scratch Bucky's withers while disciplining his voice with lightness.

"Right." Lauren glanced up at him. "Matt. Murphy."

"Is this going to be a thing with you?"

"You know it is."

"Thanks for the warning, Miss Pixie Pants."

She snorted, and then for a time, they stood in the quiet of the corral. Bucky soaked in their attention, his ears moving in a happy sort of dance while he snuffled what remained of his alfalfa before diving into the grass hay Matt had forked into the bunk.

"You're right though." Matt continued running his hand against the warm, soft fur near Bucky's neck. "Katrine texted me last night. She wants to talk."

From her profile, he could see the easy humor drain from Lauren's expression. Her lips pressed into a line, and a frown puckered her brow.

"Not a good idea though, is it?"

She stepped away from Bucky and circled to where Sheela tugged her share of the food from the opposite side of the bunk—a place from which Matt could no longer gauge Lauren's thoughts by her expression.

"Not my deal, Matt. I don't know her, and I'm not sure what you want, so…"

His chest squeezed. What did he want? Not more than three weeks before, he would have proclaimed exactly what that was without a doubt or hesitation. Hadn't he, in fact, begged God to make Katrine see how good they would be together? To just clear the path for the picture-perfect future Matt had planned?

Now? His heart wouldn't settle, and that sense of being sucked into quicksand whenever Katrine came to mind had grown stronger over the night and throughout the day. Uncertainty and a hint of regret over his stubbornness about it all permeated that downward pull.

"I'm not sure what I want either," he mumbled.

Lauren failed to respond. Matt waited, desperate for her to speak, until the extended empty space became too much.

"I blocked her number last night."

By his view of her back, her head startled up, and then she froze. "Oh?" She sounded tentative, and then cleared her throat. "Why would you do that? Maybe you two do need to talk."

With a long draw of crisp air, mildly scented by sweet alfalfa and dusted with the musk of grass hay, Matt sorted through the confusion yet again. "She said she'd needed me there—at the wedding. That's a weird thing for a bride to tell a man she wasn't marrying, don't you think?"

"Not something you'd expect." Caution painted Lauren's

response. "But maybe you're like a big brother to her or something?"

"Would a big brother's absence stop you from marrying the love of your life?"

"Maybe, if I thought he didn't approve and I respected his opinion."

"If you respected his opinion that much, you likely won't have made it all the way to the alter in a puffy white dress."

"In theory."

"Well, that theory is irrelevant, anyway. She didn't think of me like a brother."

"Men are prone to misunderstanding women. How do you know that for sure?"

Suddenly his heart pulsed with the kind of surge that came with a confession.

Lauren stepped around the bunk and, with a tipped chin, settled a curious, wide-eyed look on his face. "Matt?"

The pinch in his chest and the wash of heat on his face sure felt suspiciously like shame. Should it? Under the guise of petting Bucky's nose, he shuffled to a new position, attempting to escape Lauren's watch. "A woman doesn't kiss her brother. Usually."

A throbbing silence settled, tension uneased by the chattering of birds or a light breeze sweeping through the pine tops surrounding them.

"She kissed you?"

He cleared his throat. "Yeah. I mean, not recently." He hooked a hand around his neck. "Not while she and John were together. But I kissed her. Once."

"You kissed her, or she kissed you?"

"Uh." So stupid. Why was he talking about this with Lauren? And why did it feel like a betrayal against her to admit it? "I kissed her."

"And she..."

"Kissed me back."

He felt the release of Lauren's gaze—a relief and an ache all at once. With a glance over the horse's head, he caught the pinch of her brow before she moved back to the place she'd claimed beside Sheela.

Her obvious disappointment in him crashed over his shoulders like a wave of icy water. He wished the admission back. Maybe wished the actual incident back. While he hadn't lied—Katrine and John had been on a break two years ago when he'd tested Katrine's lips and found them willing—even then the move had felt wrong. Like disloyalty. To John. And maybe even to himself, because though he'd hoped at the time that kiss would redefine everything, he'd known better.

Over the years, Katrine had attached herself to Matt every time she and John had split. The result had been the same every time—certainly by her design. John would come back, begging for forgiveness for whatever minor infraction he'd committed, and Katrine would yield.

She'd used Matt. Every. Time. And he'd played the fool. Every. Time.

"Did you ever tell John?" Though softly spoken, Lauren's question shattered the quiet cloak that had caught Matt up in revelation.

This time he *knew* it was shame that burned his neck and face. "No."

"What about Katrine—did she?"

Had she told John? Likely, yes—and recently, if Matt's gut had any accurate instinct at all. A confession from her would explain why both parties texted him yesterday, and why John, who was usually rational with most things, blamed Katrine's flightiness on him.

Man, he was a wreck. Had he always been this messed up?

He stared, unseeing, across the corral and into the forest beyond. *Such a fool. A gullible, hardheaded sucker.*

At the warm touch of her hand on his arm, he started. Blinking, he found his focus on her upturned face. Sympathy, and not condemnation, softened those brown eyes. Still, he felt every bit the idiot he'd been.

"Jeremiah 29:11," she said, her voice kind and gentle.

"What?"

"When we've finished memorizing the verse in Isaiah, we should work on that one in Jeremiah."

He had a vague imprint of the words in his mind. Didn't nearly every Christian in western culture? It was one of those references scrawled out on at least a third of every religious graduation card handed to a freshly released senior, right?

"The plans verse?"

"That's the one." Her touch fell away.

"Seems we both already know it."

"Maybe." She leaned, nudging her shoulder into his side. "Or maybe we just know of it. That's not the same thing, is it?"

Matt studied the woman, flecks of green still littering her hat and coat, and a heart set on God becoming clearer in everything she said. Gratitude swept into the places of tumult, calming the storm with a quiet yielding—something of a developing trend settling into his reactions to her. Shifting to wrap an arm around her, he squeezed her into a side hug.

"No, I guess it's not the same thing at all."

***

I have a proposition. You could do my scheduling remotely. That way I still have someone I can trust with my appointments, and you can play at being an outdoorsy girl for the duration.

Lauren flicked the phone onto the foot of the bed and sank onto the mattress. Ashley could not take no for an answer, and her persistence stirred up bitterness. The thing was, her sister didn't actually need her. Ashley was being controlling, was all. And an attention leech. And selfish.

Lying back against the stack of pillows, Lauren shut her eyes. *Consider others above self.*

Did that mean she needed to relent? Run back at Ashley's beckon, do her every bidding?

Do not allow bitterness a foothold.

Ah. Clarity. Somehow she needed to find a way to stand in her own convictions about finding a life for herself without yielding to the toxic hold of resentment.

The word *toxic* scrawling through her thoughts shifted her mind back to the conversation she and Matt had started and left unfinished. Yes, there were toxic people in life. And no, they didn't always mean to be. Sometimes they just needed to hear an unwavering *no*.

Had Lauren ever, in her life, done that with Ashley, without it having come from a place of frustrated anger? Eesh. Too much conviction there.

Under the weight of both concern and conviction, she reached for her Bible, which waited on her nightstand. The pages opened willingly to the Psalms, the book she spent most of her evenings reading. Tracing the black letters on the smooth page, she found chapter 31 and began reading. At verse 19, she paused. Reread. Reflected.

How great is Your goodness that You have stored up for those who fear You...for those who take refuge in You.

The goodness of God, even in the struggles and disappointments of life.

Lauren turned her thoughts back to Matt. And as she turned their conversations that day, and the confusion she'd seen in his eyes and the bondage she'd read in his expression, those thoughts morphed into prayers.

Lord, guide Matt and keep him. Help him to know Your plans are for good, to give them a hope and a future. Help him to trust Your good intent for his life.

A faint echo of the same prayer whispered through her heart, only this one for herself. She reread Psalm 31, shut her eyes, and let the words of promise resonate to the marrow of her being. God's good intent was for those who feared Him.

It was more than possible that she needed to grasp that truth every bit as much as Matt.

Chapter Ten
(in which Lauren makes a mistake)

A pungent tang of saddle soap, Neatsfoot oil, and leather filled the tack room as Matt sat on an overturned bucket, working oil into the wide leather straps of the harness. The small group that had arrived two days before had requested a ride, if the snow covered enough ground. If the steady salting of the earth continued through the afternoon as it had been falling since nine that morning, the next day would be perfect for a sleigh ride.

Matt whistled while he ran a thumb over the dark, soft leather. Mr. Appleton had given him a few lessons at the reins, but even if Matt had full confidence in driving the sleigh, he wouldn't do it. Not after he'd witnessed how much Harold enjoyed the activity.

Hitching the horses, however, Matt would do. Gladly—and most certainly under the patient though particular guidance of his boss.

"Dad, Mom says lunch is being served."

The call came from somewhere on the back side of the property—likely from the ten-year-old boy who was a guest with his family. He had an older sister, and the family had rented two of the rooms. Their other guests were a newlywed couple. Adorable. No, not in a sarcastic way. The pair, clearly so in love they could hardly be separated, were honestly charming. In an annoyingly enviable sort of way.

Upon checking in yesterday, they'd gushed over the lodge and had thanked Lauren with deep enthusiasm for rescuing their honeymoon. Matt wasn't exactly sure what that meant, but he had an idea that it had something to do with Lauren's efforts in recruiting guests.

She was good for this place. For Appleton. And for himself.

Three days had gone by since he'd completely exposed his sad idiocy to Lauren. She hadn't treated him any differently. With the consistency she'd shown before, she smiled at him in the mornings when she went for a mug of coffee from the Keurig—finding him anchored to the spot he'd claimed since the first day near the fire for his morning readings. Just as steadily, she agreed to lunch when he'd come in from his morning work hungry and chilled. And as she had three days back, she went with him to the corrals to tend the horses.

Her steadfast character lent him a solid line to grab hold of in the middle of his self-imposed madness. Something of hope that, when he found the strength and courage to go back home and face those who had been witness to his role in the whole John-Katrine mess, he'd find a few loyal companions who would not hold the debacle against him for life. Certainly his parents would be among those—although seeing how right Dad had been in his concerns, and how stubbornly foolish Matt had been in his ignoring those warnings, nursed hesitancy at the thought of facing his family. But as Lauren had been tender about it—not a pushover, but kind—so would his father and mother. His brothers...

Well. Brothers were brothers, and who could change that? He'd have to man up and take the blows—the teasing jabs and the more sharp-edged cuts, as both could be expected from different siblings.

Either way, though, he wasn't quite ready to face his hometown alone. Not yet. Maybe by Thanksgiving—the day of which Mr. Appleton insisted the lodge be closed, though Lauren had suggested to him that they could charge extra the night before and night of because of the holiday, and the revenue could only help.

Mr. Appleton, with his gaze unwavering, had shaken his head. "Money is not the end all. And here's a lesson you can take to the bank—family and friends cannot be replaced. I'll not bow to the greedy demands of the dollar at the expense of relationships. Not for myself, and not for the people who work for me."

Whew. A mighty wall of conviction upheld that man. No wonder he and Dad got along so well.

"Dad!"

"Heading in now, son. Lindy and I need to return the snowshoes first."

Ah, Matt's cue. He'd be needed down at the equipment barn—their new, more client-appealing name for the machine shed, a la Lauren's suggestion. Careful to keep the straps straight, Matt hung the harness on the high hook above two saddle trees and grabbed a clean rag for his hands. Still working on removing oil residue from his fingers, he stepped from the tack room to the equipment barn and met the Sanderson duo.

Father and daughter grinned, pink cheeked and bright eyed.

"That's some view up at the crest," Mr. Sanderson said. "You can see past the bend of the cove, and the lake opens up wide and long."

"I haven't made it to that part of the hillside in quite some time. Even then, only once." Matt took the set of snowshoes from the daughter and, after fastening the buckles so they wouldn't tangle, hung them on a rack. "I'll have to make that my next destination."

"You didn't grow up here?" the girl asked.

"No, I'm from another mountain town about two hours away. But I was up there once as a teenager."

"It's sure lucky you get to stay here now, isn't it?"

He chuckled at her enthusiasm. "Sure is. I feel blessed—especially because I sort of stumbled onto the job. Think God was being exceptionally generous to me."

Neither father nor daughter responded to that particular comment, though by the exchanged glances between them, he knew it hadn't gone unnoticed.

Let your light so shine...

A verse his mother had put up in fancy script on the giant chore chalkboard she'd hung when Matt had been nine. On it she had listed their responsibilities for the day—all seven boys with three chores each. And the explicit instructions to do the work well and with a good attitude.

Let your light so shine before men that they may praise your father in heaven.

It had been far too long since he'd bothered to think about that—that how he lived and worked reflected what he believed and Whom he served. Matt wasn't sure exactly why he'd lost sight of that, but as truth settled into his heart and mind, it seemed his footing in life also gained more solid ground.

The Sandersons thanked him and left the barn, heading in for lunch. Emma had mentioned something about potato soup, and Matt's stomach put in a vote for lunch as well. He'd give it twenty minutes. Emma would be serving guests in the dining room next to the front desk, and Lauren likely would be helping. He had enough time to fill the void of firewood on the back side of the lodge, which he'd drained in the past couple of days, and then clean up.

Snow dusted his sleeves, and surely his head, by the time he stomped off the white stuff on the deck beside the front door. Inside, he stopped to remove his wet boots, and savored the warmth that touched his face and hands and inhaled the oh-so-good aroma of fresh-baked oatmeal rolls and potato soup. Was there apple crisp mingling among those scents? Grinning, he smelled again. Oh yeah...

Matt glanced toward Lauren's desk. At the sight of her bent frame, face in hands, that satisfied joy fell flat. "Lauren?"

Her head buried deeper into her palms, her fingers forking into the loose curls of her dark hair. Matt picked up his pace as he crossed the wood floor. "Hey, Miss Pixie Pants, what's going on?"

She groaned. Almost sounded like she was on the verge of tears. All inclination to tease a smile from her vanished, and he circled to her side of the desk. "Lauren?"

He curved a hand on her shoulder, and she peeked up. Misery marked her expression, tears a real threat—only a blink away from wetting her face.

He gripped her shoulder, instinct wanting to haul her into his arms. "What happened?"

"I messed up." Her voice broke, and she drew a shuddered breath. "I really messed up, Matt."

She blinked, and, yep, there was that tear. A giant drop rolled from the corner of her eye onto her nose.

"On what?" He fought the longing to run a thumb along the streak of wetness.

"Remember I told you I had two groups interested in coming the days before Thanksgiving?"

"Yes." She'd said that the day he'd told her about kissing Katrine.

"I thought that I'd told one group that I had openings the week before, and the other group that we were available that Monday through Wednesday. But I didn't. I sent them both the same dates, and they've booked them. Only we don't have enough room for both."

Oh. Oh boy. "So we're double booked?"

"Yeah. And both groups have the potential to be long-term clients. If I have to cancel one of them because I made this huge error, I'll lose not only that revenue for this year but for every year after. Mr. Appleton, the lodge—their reputation will be damaged." She slumped forward again, one elbow on the desk, and her hand jammed in her hair. "I don't do things like this, Matt. I don't make these kinds of mistakes."

Matt actually thought he could feel something tearing within his chest. Yielding to the instinct, he turned her shoulders and pulled her against his chest, wrapping both arms around her tense frame.

Those groups... Hadn't she been working on securing their business the day he'd pestered her to go out with him to feed the horses? Distracting her with mindless chatter because he hadn't wanted to think about John and Katrine and all of the mess he'd become a part of?

Yeah, that was exactly what had happened. She'd messed up because he'd been a nuisance, had been so wrapped up in himself that he couldn't see that she'd been working for the better of the lodge.

This was his doing. He couldn't let her take the fall for it.

***

Lord, I don't do things like this! What happened?

While her eyes were shut, and she valiantly fought off more tears, the panicked prayer lifted from her mind yet again. Tucked tight against Matt, his flannel soft and smelling of leather oil and wood, she let her forehead rest against his chest. His fingers tunneled into her hair, holding her head there, while his opposite hand kept a solid hold on her back.

"Listen, Lauren. Don't panic yet, okay? I have an idea."

"We can't let them sleep in the employee wing. I already looked into it—"

"What about the cabin and house?"

In the forest? She straightened, leaned back a touch. Though Matt loosened his arms to let her pry space from him, his hands remained.

"Mr. Appleton doesn't want them used."

"I can ask." He shrugged. "What would it hurt?"

"He already addressed that. Said no. You could find yourself in trouble."

Matt studied her, eyebrows pulled inward. "Let me ask, okay?"

"Why? It's my fault."

"No, it's not. If I had let you do your work instead of focusing on myself and my problems, you would have had full attention on that letter."

Her lips press together. What was he talking about? She'd just been careless. Hadn't been his fault at all.

God, I don't make these kinds of mistakes!

With a backward step, Matt's hands fell away and he turned.

"Wait." She hustled after him. "Really, Matt, it wasn't your fault, and I should handle this."

Stride pushing forward around the desk and toward the back hall, he wasn't listening. Lauren had to double-time to keep up, repeating herself as they went. Matt didn't stop until they reached Mr. Appleton's apartment by the kitchen, and even then, he didn't listen any better. Instead, he rapped on the door before glancing down at her.

"Please, Matt. I don't want to stir up more trouble. Mr. Appleton is a kind man—I'm sure he'll be fair."

"I know it." Jaw set, he nodded.

"Well, there's both my favorite new employees." Mr. Appleton's voice reached them from the direction of the kitchen before he hobbled in an appearance. "Looking for lunch?"

"Well, eventually, yes." Matt's hand settled on Lauren's lower back. "But I needed to talk to you first."

"Sure." With a limp in his turn, Mr. Appleton pivoted and waved them toward the kitchen over his shoulder. "Come sit down."

"Matt," Lauren hissed.

"Let me handle it."

"No."

"I'm not asking you, Lauren."

"What?" Since when was Matt a pushy man? She scuttled around him as soon as they cleared the doorway. "Mr. Appleton, I have to tell—"

Matt's large palm—chilly, chapped, and smelling strongly of that saddle oil—slipped over her lips. Emma, working on the other side of the island, snorted a soft chuckle, which didn't prove helpful at all.

"Mr. Appleton, I was wondering if you'd let me clean up the house and cabin on the hill."

Lauren turned her head and tipped her chin up to pin a glare on the man holding her against his side. Matt refused to meet her scowl. The chicken.

Appleton cleared his throat. "The house?"

Emma stopped cutting apples, settling a cautious but hopeful look on their boss.

"Yes, sir," Matt said. "And the cabin."

Lauren transferred her focus from Matt to Mr. Appleton, prying at Matt's fingers. Mr. Charming suddenly became Mr. Stubborn and wouldn't let her go. Appleton studied them both. Him first. Then her. Then him again. One eyebrow hitched.

"Is there a particular reason?"

A smirk glinted from Emma as she laid her knife onto the counter. "You two certainly make this place more interesting."

Oh heavens! A rush of warmth—certainly making her face crimson—spilled into her cheeks. Had Matt intentionally given the impression that they'd...

"Hold up there." His hand fell from her face and then motioned between himself and Lauren. "Not for us."

The fire on her skin blazed hotter. Now she knew exactly where she stood with him—as if there'd been any question before. But did he have to act so...appalled at the idea of her linked with him in a more, uh, personal way?

Good grief, what a disaster.

"Good work, Ralph."

His attention whipped to her. "Ralph?"

"Yeah, like Wreck-It Ralph." She tipped her head as her brows lifted. "Way to wreck it, Ralph."

"Come on, Pixie Pants." Hand on his hip, he leaned a touch into her space. Because of that personal space problem he had. While his eyes weren't exactly heated, the lightness that typified their back-and-forth interactions had vanished as well. "That's not nice."

Lauren shook her head and then turned back to the older pair playing audience to this...argument? Banter? Who knew? Or cared? Well, two people cared, and they watched with amused attention. Edit that. By the lift of her lips, Emma was amused. Mr. Appleton, though not scowling, held a long, meaningful look on Matt. Sure that in man world understanding passed between the pair, Lauren still couldn't say for certain what that was. Skip it. Didn't have any bearing on what they'd actually come into the kitchen to do.

Sliding a step away from Matt, she squared her shoulders. "Mr. Appleton, I messed up. Matt's just trying to find a solution so I feel better, but the truth is, I double booked the lodge for the week before Thanksgiving, and I feel terrible about it. The mistake could..." She swallowed and clutched her hands together in hopes that they'd stop shaking. "The groups both have the potential for long-term engagements at the lodge."

Mr. Appleton's steady gaze held on her as stillness fell over the kitchen. A mild storm passed in his expression. Lauren's heart ramped.

He's going to fire me! What will I do then?

Closing a space with one forget-your-silly-boundaries step, Matt's hand then warmed her lower back, lending her a steadiness that she wasn't sure she should need or appreciate as much as she did. "I know you told us the house hasn't been used in quite a while, but I can work on it. I have two weeks, and I can get it ready for guests. Lauren doesn't have to cancel one of the groups if we have the house and cabin available for their use."

Mr. Appleton winced, and then his attention fell to his large, gnarled hand resting on the counter. As the pause between them lengthened, his eyes fell closed, as if there was pain in his head.

"Sir, I can cancel." Wanting to reach out, to grip that big hand and take away the pain Mr. Appleton clearly felt, Lauren stepped forward. "Matt was just trying to help me, but it's okay. This was my fault."

As if he hadn't heard Lauren, Mr. Appleton remained still.

"Harold." Emma eased near him. "It's time. It's past time, don't you think?" Her work-worn hand—dry and cracked, knuckles red—slipped over his.

Another tender heartbeat passed. What had happened in that house? What tragedy had left this deep scar in a man who had proven himself kind and hospitable?

He exhaled, glanced at Emma—a sheen glazing his eyes—and then nodded. "Yes."

99

Emma's fingers curled around his in a firmer grip. "They would have wanted it used. Enjoyed. Loved. It's a good way to honor them."

Another space of ache. Then another nod. Mr. Appleton turned his face back to Lauren and Matt. "You think you can have it ready?"

Matt's hand slid up Lauren's spine and to her shoulder, where he squeezed. "I'll make it happen."

With a small bow of his lips that blended sorrow and appreciation, Mr. Appleton nodded. "Then make it happen." He squeezed Emma's hand, still curved over his, and then with that painful gait that tugged hard on Lauren's heart, he circled the island and made his way out of the kitchen.

What had they done?

"It's a good thing." Emma leaned onto her hands, palms planted on the counter. Her whisper wavered a touch. "Truly, it is. And he'll be better for it, so don't you two feel bad. Don't feel bad at all."

Chapter Eleven
(in which Matt invites Lauren for Thanksgiving)

Transformation nearly complete. Thank You, Lord.

Lauren sank onto the cushions of the wood and leather sofa, inhaling the mingling scents of Pine-Sol, wood polish, fresh paint, vinegar, and a touch of crisp apple a la the diffuser she'd plugged in at five.

Five. That'd been over six hours before, when she'd made her way up the becoming-well-used trail from the main lodge to the original house after her early supper. It'd become habit over the past fourteen days, as she wasn't about to let Matt work on this massive reno/clean-up project on his own, not after the stumble she'd taken that had made the project necessary.

In her mind, she'd dubbed this home *Together, with Love*, a title that had come easily to her after Emma had entrusted her with the sacred story of its purpose and later neglect.

"Harold had a son. Stephen." Emma settled onto a stool beside Lauren, sliding a mug of cider toward her before wrapping both hands around her own warm drink. "He was going to take over the lodge so that Harold could focus on caring for Jane during her battle with cancer. The plan had been beautiful and a testament to the way Harold and Jane had functioned as a family. Together, with love. But then there was an accident.

"Stephen and his wife were coming back from a trip, traveling *a country highway, when an oncoming car crossed the double yellows. They were hit head on. No one survived. Texting. The other driver had been texting.*

"Harold and Jane were devastated, and worse, as they grieved their only child, Jane's health worsened. She died a year, almost to the day, after their son.

"Harold closed the house and the cabin he'd commissioned for Stephen and his wife. He moved into the first-floor apartment, and to my knowledge, hasn't stepped foot in the home where he'd raised his son and lost his wife."

Lauren sat in stunned, grieving silence, blinking against warm moisture. So tragic. Why would God allow such heartache to touch a man like Harold Appleton? Instead of voicing that unknowable question, she turned her thoughts back to Emma.

"So sad," she whispered. "They were close, weren't they?"

Emma nodded, her tears slipping unchecked. "Very close."

"And I would suspect Stephen was a good man, like his dad."

"He was. A good man. A good husband." Emma choked on that last word.

Suddenly, Lauren knew Emma's connection to Harold Appleton went much deeper than long-standing employment. "And you, Emma? Were you close to Stephen as well?"

Expression crumbling into soul-deep sorrow, Emma nodded. Her shoulders shook silently, and then she sniffed. "He married my daughter, Lauren. And they were very happy."

The blade had become double edged, and Lauren could not help the quivering of her own chest as the tears flowed freely. Where there were no words, there was presence. She slipped off her stool and cradled the woman at her side.

"They loved this place. That home. That cabin." After a time, Emma withdrew from Lauren's arms and then gripped her hands. "It's sat abandoned, like a hopeless tomb, for far too long. I know you and Matt will honor them with this project, and I'm grateful."

She'd never been entrusted with something so sacred. The weight of it sank in deep, but not as a burden. This was what she had craved before, to be a part of something that involved so much more than her intellect. Something that moved with meaning deep within, to the depths of her core.

Together, with Love.

Lauren sighed, leaning back into the plush cushion as it

creaked, the way old leather did, while enveloping her with welcomed softness. Her arms and back ached from scrubbing, and her hands had quickly morphed to resemble Emma's. Not bad things. Not bad at all. As her eyes slipped shut, her mouth curved in satisfaction.

Oh, but she was tired!

Warmth cradled her as fatigue tugged her in deeper. *Just a few minutes*, she thought. *Just a few minutes to rest my eyes.* Her mind drifted, consciousness wavered in the pleasant darkness behind her lids. They did it—got the house and cabin done. Given the length of neglect and the work that had been required, her long exhale of relief had been well earned. Yes, they'd done it—and not a moment too soon. Her two large groups would be checking in the following morning.

When the cushion beside her crackled and then moved, her weight shifted as a presence larger than herself sank into the seat beside her. Identifying Matt was easily done, not just because he was the only other person in the house but by that enamoring scent of his. All pine and woodsman, wood smoke and working man. She let the pull of gravity roll her head toward his shoulder until her nose touched the soft fabric of his flannel.

I could get used to this.

Careful there. Somewhere in the back recesses of her mind, the warning chided. Lauren was too tired and content to take heed.

Matt's frame sank farther into the cushion beside hers, and his long sigh mirrored what she felt inside. The sweet, exhausted victory of a job completed. It'd been hard work, especially since he did it on top of all the other daily chores he had to do around the lodge. Every night for the past week and a half, in fact, he'd spent up here fixing things, redoing things, painting things, moving things.

Saving her backside. Bless him for that.

"The bathroom is painted. Last of the brushwork, I think."

She hummed an acknowledgment. "My hero."

His deep chuckle tingled her spine as his shoulder pressed into her gently. A shift of his weight, and his head leaned on hers, and then he hooked his arm—the one opposite her—over her head to settle on her, his fingers tangling in her hair.

If she wasn't so tired—and happy—she would move. Probably.

Oh, but she *could* get used to it, his nearness. The warmth seeping from his body into hers. That touch.

A lull drifted around them, full of comfortable silence with a subtle hint of *what if*. Well, for her there was that hint.

"Lauren?" Her name on his voice came soft and low.

"Yeah?"

"Who's Ashley?"

"Hmm?" A strange question, straight out of the blue.

"Ashley. She's the one who texts you in the evenings, right? The one who makes you scowl."

Lauren tried to sit up, but his hand held fast, fist gripping her hair. She hadn't any true desire to move, so she settled her cheek more comfortably on his shoulder. "I don't scowl."

"I could take a picture next time, but then you'd owe me."

"What would I owe you?"

This time he hummed a response, the low sound from his throat setting off a prickle along her hair. Maybe she needed to listen to that warning still nagging in the back of her mind.

"An undetermined favor," he finally said.

"That sounds like a bad setup, Matt Murphy."

"Matthew Murphy."

"Matt. Murphy."

He sighed, sending a current of warm breath skimming across her forehead. For several breaths he didn't speak, and she wondered if he'd drifted into sleep.

Ah, so tempting.

"I've spilled my guts to you, Lauren. Fair's fair."

A breathy chuckle left her mouth. "Is that what you're worried about?"

"Who is Ashley, and why does she make you unhappy?"

This time, it was her turn to sigh. "She's my sister, and she doesn't make me unhappy. She just won't accept this move—this decision I've made to break away from her life and goals."

"That sounds complicated."

"It is. I'm too tired—and too happy about making this house work—to get into it tonight."

"Fair enough." The grip he'd taken on her hair eased, and then his fingertips brushed her neck.

Oh goodness. A shiver traveled from the thrill of his touch down the length of her arm. What was he doing?

Did she care?

Heartbroken. The man was heartbroken, and a bit of a mess about Katrine. Do you really want to be the rebound?

No. She didn't. However, she didn't exactly feel like moving from this cozy little situation either.

We can be friends like this. Some friends do this snuggling thing. Right?

Sure. Just go on ahead and feed that pretense. No danger there at all.

He'd said friends. Promised friends.

And so had she.

"I have an idea."

The sleepy sound of his voice made her want to erase the word *friends* from their agreement and find something more, uh, intimate with which to replace it. Which meant she had to work at keeping casual in her tone.

"What's that?"

"You come home with me on Thursday. For Thanksgiving."

Behind her closed eyelids, lights flashed, and a pleasant sort of dizziness made her feel...swoony?

Ugh. No. She was not a swoony kind of girl. With a palm against his warm chest—and no, she didn't notice the firmness beneath that flannel shirt—she pushed herself away from his arm, blinking sleepiness from her eyes. With a peek up, she found him watching her, the arm he'd slung over his head to tangle his fingers in her hair slowly rising to go back to his side.

She sat up. "Why?"

"Your family is on the other side of the continent. What else will you do?"

"Stay here with Emma and Harold." Her boss had asked her

one evening last week, when he'd limped himself up the path to see the progress on the house, to call him Harold. The request felt like a sacred privilege.

Matt held an unbroken study on her, the exhaustion in his gaze mingling with an intensity that seemed like a plea.

"Tell me why you want me to go, Matt."

A distance entered his expression—hesitation. Then, "Protection."

Though not intended as a jab, a prick sank unmercifully deep in her chest. "What?"

His look fell away, chin turned down and to the side. "I don't want to run into Katrine by myself."

Oh. That prick turned to a hard pinch in her heart. She should have known. Guessed. Should have listened a little more obediently to that warning in the back of her mind.

Matthew Murphy was not available for romance. Not to her. And, to be fair, he had said *friends* from the beginning, so...

Inhale. Exhale. She could still breathe. She was fine. They were fine.

"You don't trust her, or you don't trust yourself?" The question bit on the harsh side, and Lauren felt a twinge of guilt when he winced.

"Both." He pulled himself away from the cushions, turning to face her squarely as he caught her gaze again. Sincerity filled those dark eyes, and she knew she'd say yes even before he made the next statement.

"I'm stronger with you at my side, Lauren. You're good for me. You make me better at being the man I want to be."

Her lips parted as she stared at him. Mind blank, she had no idea what to say.

A friend would say yes.

But...

Yeah, there was a big *but* in there, because she'd let her imagination spark a longing that was bound to get her hurt.

"Lauren?"

She scooted off the couch. "I think we should head back now.

It's late."

"Is that a *no*?" He stood, his scent, his warmth...all of him too close.

"No, it's an *I'm tired* and *I'm not thinking clearly*." She gripped his hand—*Why? Stop with the touching!* "I'll get back to you, okay?"

Later that night, tucked snug under her flannel sheets and plush comforter, she pushed away the lingering scent of Matthew Murphy, the remnant tingle from the feathered touch he'd brushed along her neck. So she could think clearly.

Putting aside the way his compliment had made her heart roll with some kind of sweet pain, how could she possibly turn him down?

A friend wouldn't.

***

Matt knew himself to be a wimp—especially when it came to Katrine. But the engraving in his mind of Lauren's response when he'd told her he didn't want to run the risk of meeting Katrine knifed a new sense of unworthiness. He'd disappointed her—possibly hurt her? Was he the kind of man who used a woman to get back at another woman?

That blade sliced deep, and guilt oozed forth.

But I want her to go, God. I meant what I told her—I'm better with her.

The plea left off motives. And worse, failed to seek God's wisdom. Just, *This is what I want, and how about You bless it?*

There it was again—that sense that right there, in that habit, that pattern, was something he needed to confront within himself, and he needed to deal with before God. Hanging his head forward, the fire at his side snapping and his open Bible waiting on his lap, Matt shut his eyes.

Is this what I do? What I've always done?

Before the prayer could turn to conversation, the spit-gurgle-squeak of the Keurig drew his attention toward the dining room across the space. Lauren, in her cream sweater, dark jeans, and tall boots, stood in front of the coffee machine, rolling her neck from side to side.

Signs of a long night. *Good job on that, Matt.*

Leaving the book open, he slid his Bible from his lap to the seat beside him and stood. While arcing his back in a stretch, he padded in his wool socks across the gleaming wood floor and through the arched doorway into the dining room. The Keurig spit its last bit of steamy coffee as Matt stepped beside Lauren.

"Morning." She delayed her glance up to him, and when it finally made the climb so their eyes met, he found a forced smile carving her lips.

"Good morning." He pivoted so that his backside faced the coffee bar, making a careful survey of her expression. Tricky, since between that giant not-normal smile and her attention darting everywhere but on him, he couldn't get a solid read.

Lauren paid specific, careful attention to her daily doctoring practice with her coffee. As if she'd never done it before. As if it were volatile chemistry. When she finally had the precise ratio of cream-to-bold blend measured and stirred, the cap securely in place, the sipper hole angled exactly ninety degrees from the mug handle...

Good heavens. Lauren was type A, but never this over the OCD top. Matt slid a step nearer and cupped her elbow, the thick weave of her sweater soft in his palm.

She paused.

"Lauren."

"Yep?" Before the word was out, she had that very-carefully-constructed coffee at her lips.

"I put you in a bad spot. I'm sorry."

Finally. Those sweet eyes settled on his. Then she blinked. Looked at her hands. Then the floor. "It's not a big deal, Matt. I get it."

"I made you feel...awkward."

"I was just tired. Told you, wasn't thinking straight."

"But—"

"Matt, I'm a grown-up girl, and I can handle this. Because I'm your friend. You don't need to feel bad, and I'm happy to go with you for Thanksgiving. If you still want me to."

Matt leaned against the counter, a battle of contradictions warring for primacy in his emotions. He was thankful—for her friendship and her willingness to be a go-between in this for him. On the opposite side of that, humiliation pulled hard and heavy. What kind of a man was he anyway? Couldn't face a girl he'd thought he'd loved, so his solution was to drag along another woman?

And what about this other woman, the one right in front of him? Meeting her had been like breathing in clean mountain air after being stuck in the city during a particularly smoggy week. Like a clear dawning of new day after a long, stormy night. She laughed and worked with equal zeal. Respect and compassion flowed freely into her words and her actions. Her knowledge of God proved to be both academic and practice.

Lauren had been as much healing to his distress as she had been a godsend to this struggling lodge, with it's admirable, elderly owner and unmet potential.

And Matt? He'd invited her home as a distraction and shield, taking advantage of her generous friendship.

Nice.

"Matt?" Lauren tipped her head as she called him back to the present.

"Yeah, sorry."

"Do you still want me to come?"

That concoction of disagreeable emotions stirred again. Even still, as he caught her face in his glance, the genuineness of her offer, the sweetness of her presence gripped harder.

"Yes," he said. "Yes, I do."

He wanted to hug her when a soft bow moved her lips. Gone was the falseness that she'd worn so unnaturally before. There, in that honeyed grin, was his friend.

And he was grateful.

Chapter Twelve
(in which Lauren meets the Murphy boys)

"Tell me what I need to know." Lauren snapped the seat belt secure and settled in for the drive ahead. Matt had said a couple of hours, give or take. With the flakes drifting from the sky, increasing in rate and size, she guessed it would be more of a *give* situation this trip.

Which was okay. Nerves danced in her stomach with all the pleasantness of an internal mosquito invasion. She'd never gone to a man's house to meet his family. Not once. Never had dated anyone seriously enough to make it worth that kind of pressure.

Then again, she and Matt weren't dating.

Be gone, then, pesky anxieties.

"What do you want to know?" Matt had the four-wheel-drive Escape in gear and pointed down—or rather, up—the road. They had to climb a pass, descend into a valley, cross it, and take on another pass to reach the Murphy residence. The journey sounded treacherous in those terms. Also, she'd learned on friendship-with-Matt-day-one that *four-wheel drive* in his world meant more likely to get *really* stuck because of the perceived invincibility factor.

Ahem. Matt disagreed with that assessment.

Perhaps these traveling fears were the real bait for those worry skeeters. Not at all the idea of meeting Matt's family.

Just keep telling yourself that...

Lauren hushed the silent conversation in her head because it was totally distracting from her attempt at distraction. "Seven brothers?"

"Six brothers. Seven boys, with me. I'm the oldest." Matt leaned back, casual as you please, unbothered by the wet roads, falling temperatures, and snow gathering on the edges of the pavement. "After me, there's Jacob—we call him the Ambitious. He's married to Kate, but don't ask about the wedding. It's tricky, because she used to date Jackson, who is the middle brother, and known as the Clown. In between Jacob and Jackson, there's Connor—known to us as the Constant. He's an officer in the army. Went through ROTC in high school and two years of college and then went full time with the army."

He hooked an arm over the back of her seat. She tried not to notice much.

"Jacob, Jackson, Connor," she said, tapping her fingers against her jeans with each name.

"No, Jacob, Connor, Jackson."

"*J, C, J*. Got it. And no *M* names. But we've already been over that."

His knuckle brushed her cheek with a bit of a push behind the touch. "Miss Pixie Pants. Better bring it, lady. My brothers will eat it up like Mom's homemade pizza."

"That sounds ominous."

He smirked. "I'll protect you."

"Right." She pinned a raised-brow look on him.

"You won't need it." He snickered.

"Because they'll be nice?"

"Of course they'll be nice. Murphy boys are always nice. Just, kind of ornery in our niceness."

"You know that's a contradiction, don't you?"

"And true just the same."

A small laugh escaped before she could discipline it. "Okay. That's four boys, including you. Give me the rest."

"Sure you can handle it?"

"Think it's too late if I can't."

"True. So we stopped at Jackson. The middle. The Clown. But wait. You have to take some notes on him."

"Uh, yikes?"

"Nah, he's hilarious. Even works some stand-up on the side. He's an electrician by trade though. But here's what you need to know—he's a total prankster. Doesn't care if you've just met or even if he knows your name. You can bank on him having something up his sleeve. So. Watch out."

Unease and curiosity played Ping-Pong in her stomach. "Pranks? Like what?"

"Hmmm...let me think of some of his more famous jobs." He snapped, chuckling at whatever he was about to share. "Several years ago he convinced our youngest brother, Brayden—the Tenderheart—that he'd made him invisible. Had all of us boys in on it. Told him he'd learned a new magic trick and could make him invisible. Brayden was only six at the time, and Jackson was in high school, so it wasn't too hard to convince him. At first the kid thought it was cool. But then, as the day wore on and we basically ignored Bray, he wasn't so excited. By the day's end, he was in tears, begging Jackson to make him un-invisible."

"Aww, that's mean! Poor kid."

"Yeah, he and my parents had a chat about taking things too far and respecting other people's dignity. Jackson ended up feeling really bad about it. He won't pull anything like that anymore."

"Are you sure? Because, now I'm scared." Like she wasn't scared before. This guy sounded like a total meanie.

"Naw. Don't worry about it. Jackson's got a good heart. And he's been through some stuff. But like I said, don't bring that up. Nothing will shut him down faster."

She tapped her lips, taking in the scenery as it passed by. Thick stands of trees, mostly, drooping heavily with snow. "Okay, I'll remember."

They rounded the final switchback of the pass, cresting the climb. The view opened between a stand of pines and the fold of a neighboring mountain, revealing the sprawl of a wide valley below, bisected by a wandering river. Lauren caught her breath, and the words of Psalm 95 scrawled through her mind.

For the Lord is the great God, the great King above all gods. In his hand are the depths of the earth, and the mountain peaks belong to him.

"How much of the Bible do you have in that memory?"

Startled, Lauren jerked her gaze back to Matt. "What?"

"That was a verse, right? I'd guess from the Psalms." His focus on the road, she watched the corner of his eye crinkle with his grin.

He's so handsome with that easy smile. How had Katrine missed it? Also, did I say that verse out loud?

What else had she said out loud and not realized it?

That was a big old *yikes!* Because there were thoughts in her head—specifically about Matt—that should *not* be spoken.

"Are you going to make me guess?" he asked.

She leaned into the door as the first hairpin turn down the pass shifted her body. "No. It's Psalm Ninety-Five verse four."

"Psalm Ninety-Five verse four. I'll add that to the list."

"The list?"

"Yeah, of verses to memorize. Trying to catch up to you, you know."

No. She didn't know. Although that news was mildly interesting, in a good way. "It's not a competition."

"Right. Just good for me, is what it is."

Oh. She definitely liked that.

"You challenge me, you know that, right? That's one of the ways you're good for me. My mom, she always had a verse of the week for us boys to work on. And Dad, he started every day in the Bible. Without fail."

"Like father, like son."

A brush of color feathered his cheekbones. "Yeah, well, I might have neglected that practice. Until recently."

Hmmm... She'd seen him every morning, set in that chair beside the fire, Bible open, head bowed. Had he only stepped into that habit when they'd started at the lodge?

"Tyler is next. Tyler-Tarzan." Matt's random comment cut into her thoughts.

Sheesh, he was hard to keep up with sometimes. "Say that again?"

"Tyler. He's the next brother, after Jackson. We call him Tyler-Tarzan. He's fearless and a monkey, which proves helpful when roofing. He's in college right now. CalTech."

"Explains your abundance of CalTech T-shirts."

Those smile crinkles reappeared. Had anyone ever recorded the attractiveness of smile crinkles? They were definitely noteworthy. Or maybe that was just Matt's?

Goodness, if she didn't get these random thoughts under control, this was going to be a long, sit-on-the-razor-edge-of-saying-something-irrevocable four days. *God, please help me rein in this attraction. I really do want to be the friend Matt needs. And also not humiliate myself with him.*

"Okay, Tyler. Then who?" she said.

"Then come the two babies of the family—both still in high school. You can remember their names by *b is for baby*, as in Brandon and then Brayden. Brayden the Tenderheart—who is the baby of the family and loves it. And Brandon the Bold. Kid has had a hard time using a filter on his mouth."

"B is for baby?" She smirked, and he caught it. "Should I tell them you said that?"

"Well, you could. But you'd be subjected to a round of bellyaching and then a show of brotherly wrestling, which is never tame. And yours truly will win."

"Ah." She tipped her head back and laughed. "Is that so?"

"So."

"Humble much?"

"Just honest."

She turned in her seat, shoulder punching into the back. "This you might have to prove."

"Any day, Pixie Pants."

"You can't call me that in front of your family."

A mischievous glint danced in his eyes as he chanced a glance toward her.

She pointed at the road. "Eyes forward. And promise me you

won't embarrass me."

That hand that had been ever near her—on her seatback or on the console between them—clutched at his heart. "How could you even?"

She snorted. "How could I not, Matt Murphy?"

"We've discussed the name thing."

"Yes." She held a steady look of warning on him. "We have. So promise."

That lighthearted, laugh-the-trip-away look faded from his profile, and his hand fell toward her again. Covering her fingers, he squeezed. "I promise you, Lauren. I'll not embarrass you, and I won't let my brothers go too far. You're safe with me."

Warmth pooled in her chest at that last statement, followed quickly by an uncomfortable squeeze in the same place. *Matt the Heartbroken.* She couldn't grab on to these moments of depth with Matt, as though they were a foundation on which to build something more than friends. Doing so simply wasn't safe, no matter what Matt claimed.

"What does your family call you?" She'd latch on to his character name given by his people, because she couldn't call him Matt the Heartbroken out loud. That wouldn't go over well.

"The Mountain Man."

"Because of your size or the fact that you love the outdoors?"

"Yes." He dropped a wink.

Tempted as she was to stare at that crinkled-eyed, good-looking profile, sitting all large and warm next to her, Lauren focused on the scenery around them. A quaint mountain village dotted the valley, nearly as picturesque as something she would imagine the Painter of Light would brush onto a canvas. Cozy farmhouses mixed with sturdy cabins peppered the banks of the wandering river, separated by snow-blanketed fields and stands of evergreens.

A flash of a scene—lovely and perfect—blipped through her mind. Her, living in the idyllic valley, in one of those charming homes, a ribbon of smoke drifting from the stone chimney and an *un*heartbroken M—

No. Daydreaming such things would never prove helpful. *Dwell on things that are true.*

As the road leveled into the valley, straightening as they continued forward, Lauren leaned her head against the seat and shut her eyes. Nerves and longings, both of which she'd worked hard to bury, wore on her.

"Will you get car sick on the next pass if I let you sleep?" Genuine concern laced Matt's voice.

"Before the last flight I took, I would have said no." She yawned. "But, now... I really don't want to throw up on you again." Repositioning in her seat, she blinked, trying to remove the craving to sleep.

Matt brushed his palm over her eyes. "Sleep. There's twenty minutes of flat ahead of us. I'll wake you up when we start the next pass."

She rolled her head to look at him, finding his gaze already on her. "Promise?"

He reached behind his seat, snagged his heavy winter coat that had been stowed there, and pushed it into her lap. "Promise."

Within minutes after arranging his coat—which smelled deliciously of him—as a pillow, she drifted off, scenes of that pleasant valley daydream stubbornly etched in her mind.

***

Matt glanced at her face. The soft lines, peaceful expression, and natural curve on her lips. Even in her sleep, she possessed a joy that radiated through her presence.

It called to him. *Come, taste.*

Her? Or that joy?

Both?

Don't mess with Lauren.

Mr. Appleton's warning sliced through his musings. Setting him straight again. No, he would not mess with Lauren. He wasn't the type of man to mess with any woman's heart. Still, a thrill rushed through him that she was right there, beside him.

Going home with him.

He wasn't willing to examine that thrill deeper, lest he find a need to discipline it. Instead, he let it settle. Linger. Dwell.

***

Upon entering the Murphy home, Lauren had immediately been introduced to Helen, Matt's mom. The matriarch of such a large clan didn't look anything like Lauren had imagined. Where she'd pictured a plump woman, hair cut short and possessing Matt's dark eyes, and perhaps a grandmotherly air, reality revealed a woman whose athletic build suggested she might be able to work right alongside her oldest son—the Mountain Man—and never get winded. Her long hair, twisted into a loose braid, was a weave of sandy brown and silver, which lent a confident wisdom to her attractiveness, like she felt no need to try to look like she was in her twenties because she liked just fine the decade she'd attained to in life. She smiled as readily as her boys, and joy danced in her pale-blue eyes.

Lauren liked her immediately.

"Make yourself at home—if you can with this litter of boys who tromp through my house." Helen gave her a side hug.

"Thank you." Lauren looked around the house with appreciation. It felt a bit like the lodge, actually, with the vaulted ceiling and wide-open spread of the open-concept space. However, Helen preferred the trending farmhouse style, as cream dominated the color scheme, softening the stone fireplace and the large wood beams supporting the ceiling.

Lauren smiled back at her hostess. "May I start with a restroom?"

"Absolutely." Helen pointed toward a long hallway.

Matt turned from his lively conversation with Jackson, hand up. "Hang on. Let me check it first."

Helen chuckled. "Good idea."

They both looked at Jackson.

"What?" He held both palms up. "I just got here too."

"Thirty minutes ago." Helen quirked a knowing challenge at her middle son. "Thirty minutes is plenty of time for you to find some way to make trouble. Remember the goldfish last Easter?"

Jackson's eyes lit with laughter, but his grin remained tame. "What? I made sure the water bottle was transparent."

"I missed this one." Matt turned an interested look on his brother, who merely shrugged.

"That's what happens when you don't come home," Jackson said. "You miss stuff."

Lauren turned to Helen. "What happened to the goldfish?"

"My son, who thinks he's clever, came home for Easter and put two goldfish in Brandon's large water bottle and then stuck it in the fridge. Brandon didn't notice until he got to the gym."

"Oh! Yuck!" Lauren twisted her face into a grimace.

"Dude, that's gross." Matt's laughter overrode his words.

Again, Jackson shrugged, but his smile broke wide open.

"On that note, I'm on bathroom inspection." Squeezing Lauren's shoulder as he passed, Matt moved down the hallway.

"I'm actually harmless." Jackson's grin remained playful and was made unique by the scar on his upper lip. Clearly this man had mastered charm, which could be dangerous to the female population—enough to make Lauren cautious of him, if not for the fact that Matt had said his prankster brother had a good heart.

Within a minute of disappearing, Matt sauntered back toward the group, a roll of toilet paper in his hand. "Really, Jackson?" He tossed the offending item at the man who shared his dark hair and eyes but not quite his build. "Packing tape? You've done that one before. Running out of ideas?"

Jackson twisted his mouth. "Aw, nuts." There was that charm again, all mischievous boy and innocent trouble. The very one that had probably kept him alive for his twenty-some years. He tossed the roll into the air and caught it. "It was worth another go."

"Undo it." Matt crossed his arms.

Jackson whipped a pocketknife from his jeans and sliced through the first quarter inch of the paper, including the clear tape he'd wrapped around it. With a theatrical bow, he passed the now-free roll to Lauren. "Your very own pristine, unfettered roll of TP. Guard it well, my lady."

"For real," Matt muttered and then shoved his brother. "She just got here. You're going to scare her off."

Jackson straightened. "She rode up with you over two passes. I doubt she's that skittish."

"I'm an excellent driver."

"That's what all bad drivers say."

Matt hooked his hands on his hips. "Tell him, Lauren. Tell my knucklehead brother what an excellent driver I am."

"Uh..."

The brothers began an elbow-jabbing battle, instigated by Jackson, who rolled his head back and laughed when Lauren didn't defend Matt.

"Oh, stop, you clowns. No wonder Kate doesn't want to spend the holidays with us." Words barely out, Helen froze, her eyes flying to Jackson.

The elbow war ceased.

"I'm sorry, son," Helen whispered.

Jackson shoved his hands into his pockets, the playfulness draining from him with the speed of water from a broken dam. He turned his head, looked toward the kitchen on his right, and then shrugged. "That's a nice arrangement, Mom." He pointed to a large fall bouquet on the counter. "Is the pumpkin real?"

Discomfort seeped from Helen as she watched Jackson move toward the other room. "I don't know what I was thinking."

Matt closed the gap between him and his mom, speaking low. "He's fine, Mom. Don't worry about it."

Her mouth twisted to one side.

"Seriously," Matt said. "The best thing you can do for him is to let it go."

Chapter Thirteen
(in which Matt discovers a woman who fears the Lord is to be praised)

She's definitely the kind of girl you take home to meet your mother.

Connor's comment, spoken quietly in the bunkroom the four older boys shared, repeated through Matt's mind while his family's home settled into the silence of night. His brother had intended the words as a compliment—and truly they were.

Though some scoffed at that type of evaluation, thinking for some unidentifiable reason that the kind of woman you'd want your mother to meet was uninteresting, Matt couldn't think of anything better than having his parents approve of a woman he was interested in. He knew that for a fact, because they *hadn't* approved of Katrine. Not when they'd figured out he'd gone dumb-puppy over her and she...

She what?

Skip it. He'd been sick of thinking about Katrine. Wondering if she missed him, or if she'd gone back to John. Wondering if she had spent the past several weeks figuring out how to get ahold of him since he'd blocked her number. Wondering, even fearing, that she'd show up in Sugar Pine over Thanksgiving—which wouldn't be a normal move for her, since she disdained the small *prosaic* town. However, Katrine was also unrelenting when it came to the pursuit of what she wanted, so if she wanted to talk to him, she'd be back.

Which edged him past worried and toward terrified.

That was an interesting—no alarming—reaction. In all that wondering about Katrine, Matt had also spent many late-night hours examining himself. Asking some hard questions, and not really finding comfort in the shadowy answers.

Had he really loved Katrine?

The uncertainty he felt with that question now made him a little sick. For years he'd been...infatuated? Yes. Maybe even more than that. Obsessed? Man, that felt creepy. But it fit. Not in the scary-stalker way, but in an unhealthy-addiction sort of way, and touching the edges of that understanding disturbed him. Deeply.

Especially when he was brave enough to look back on who he'd become as he'd attempted to gain all that he'd wanted.

I just don't think she's good for you, son.

His mother's words, delivered gently but with a clear expression of loving concern. That had been three years back, when he'd told his dad that he'd rethought the father-son partnership they'd talked about since he'd been eighteen. He'd loved working with his dad. Loved being outside, doing something creative and gratifying and physically demanding. Had been more than good enough for him, whether the payout had been big or small—and they'd done both kinds of jobs.

But then...Katrine.

He'd moved to the city, where smog, crowds, and stuffy office work consumed him. Because she'd told him she could never be with a man who couldn't make real bank working a real job. She and John had been on a break at the time, and it had seemed like things were finally falling into place for Matt...

Sacrifice was part of relationship. That was what he'd told himself and his parents. They agreed, except he didn't actually have a relationship with Katrine. He had a twisted version of dependency that had grown claws, gripped his soul, and was morphing him in ways they'd found alarming. Like him abandoning work he enjoyed. And neglecting important things like family, church, and personal study.

Lying in bed, Matt rubbed his forehead.

Lord, I've been a mess. His nose began to sting. *Such a mess, and I'm not sure my head and heart are right yet. But Lauren...*

What about Lauren?

She was the kind of woman you brought home to meet your mother. The kind of woman who poured in more than she sucked out of the people around her. The kind who made him want to be a better person—better friend, better son, better Christian.

A woman who fears the Lord is to be praised.

He couldn't name the reference, but he knew that was from the Bible. And Lauren Matlock...

She fit.

***

Lauren sank into the large, unusually comfortable bed.

"The guest room," Helen had said. "Untouched by my unmarried sons because who really wants to sleep where a former ten-year-old boy had once laid his unwashed stinky self?"

Entirely enchanted with this large family, specifically by this hospitable and humorous woman, Lauren had laid her head back and laughed.

"I imagine Matt would argue that with you," she'd said.

"Ah. You've picked up on my son's tendency toward self-defense?" Helen had winked and then reached for Lauren's hand. "But he has his virtues too."

"That he does," Lauren had agreed, although she hadn't ever considered Matt to be defensive. Ah well. Mothers saw things friends often didn't. At least Helen didn't seem to think her baby boy was Prince Charming stepping out of the page, infallible and unmatched.

The not so distant conversation drifted leisurely through her mind as she snuggled under the thick red-pinstriped duvet. The bed smelled of peppermint, which contrary to intuition, invited Lauren to shut her eyes and drift upon sweet dreams. A satisfied smile played at her lips as she surrendered to the gentle bidding of the night.

Stepping into the Murphy home had been a bit like going to the fair. Lots of noise—laughter a dominant echo, largely thanks to Jackson—good smells of mouthwatering food, and more to watch than Lauren could take in. Growing up as a politician's daughter, Lauren had seen her share of crowds, but at home there had been only her parents and Ashley along with her, and none of them had been the overtly demonstrative or loud types.

Truthfully, the Murphy gathering had been a touch overwhelming. But only because the constant movement and buzz of multiple conversations was foreign to her homelife. In spite of the sense that she'd walked into a small circus, she found herself easily liking Matt's family. Those she'd met in the first evening, anyway. Jacob and his wife, Kate, didn't make an appearance. Something about deciding against taking the time off.

Jackson, however, had been there and, as promised, proved to be an eternal goofball.

The earlier bathroom prank reran, provoking a quiet chuckle. Ah, Jackson. So clever, throwing his brother off with a prank he'd already pulled before. Never mind that Jackson's trick had cost her a dry backside and smidge of her dignity. It had been funny. The memory of the clear saran wrap catching what was supposed to go into the toilet bowl and splashing her exposed seat, and her unhindered shouted response—*Jackson!*—grew that chuckle into a fit of giggles.

"What did you do?" Matt's boom came from the hallway, nearing the bathroom door with every word.

Jackson's bellow of laughter rang out clear, right before a scuffle of bodies, the sound of boys shoving and landing against the walls. Lauren grinned, confident the row was of the playful variety.

"Don't kill him, Matt," she called.

"Are you sure, Lauren? There are five others enough like him that it won't matter much."

"Hey!" Jackson played offended well. Not surprising. "You'd be bored to death without me."

Lauren dared to join the banter. "My backside would be dry without you, so there is that."

"Dude!" Matt's tone turned a degree toward serious. "What did you do?"

"Nothing a quick shower won't fix." Next, Jackson's voice edged toward worried. "You're not too mad, right, Lauren? You came home with my brother, so you've got to be a pretty decent sport." A hesitation. Then, "Right?"

She held quiet, enjoying the moment of imagining Matt's younger brother squirm. He deserved it.

"Lauren?" Jackson again, and yes, he was positively worried.

"Bro, I'm gonna—"

Lauren busted with laughter, cutting off Matt's threat.

"Lauren, are you okay?"

"Yeah, I'm fine." She snickered. "Just need a quick rinse. And then I'm pretty sure Jackson will need to clean the toilet."

"With his toothbrush," Matt responded.

"After that, he can take care of my bag," Lauren continued. "And then warm my boots by the fire. And I think I need a mug of hot cocoa. You know how to make a mug of hot cocoa, right Jackson?"

Though his laughter sounded similar to Matt's, Lauren could tell that it was Jackson's relieved response wafting from the hall. "I do. And I can do that. Anything else?"

"I think that will suffice," Lauren answered smugly.

"Are there towels in there, or should I go hunt some down?"

She glanced around, finding a rolled set of fluffy cream and brown towels in a basket near the shower. "I think I'm set."

"Take your time, Lauren," Matt said, his voice fading as he moved away from the door. "I'm going to take my brother out for a walk. Apparently he needs it."

Thus, the weekend began. Eventful, but not bad.

Lying there, clean and warm in the plush guest bed hours after that eventful introduction, Lauren wondered at how comfortable she'd become with a group of men who were so much different from her own family. A rather serious bunch, her people. Matt's... Well. There she had it—within ten minutes of meeting them, she'd needed a shower.

But oh, the laughter they'd shared throughout the evening, and not just Jackson—although he was certainly entertaining with his gift for humorous storytelling and propensity for mischief. But Kevin—Matt's dad—and Helen, as well as the brothers who were there, all genuinely loved to laugh, and enjoyed each other.

Probably explained why Matt didn't freak out when they'd first met and she'd puked all over his suit. And wasn't she eternally thankful for that?

Smile still stretched full, gratitude making her heart light, Lauren let her eyes slide shut and mind fade toward sleep.

Yes. She was quite thankful that Thanksgiving.

For Matt.

Jennifer Rodewald

Chapter Fourteen
(in which Matt has a heart-to-heart with his dad)

The group stomped the snow from their boots and gators at the back stoop behind the large greenhouse addition. The flat flagstone patio worked in the winter as their cold-weather gear collection point, and Jackson gathered the sets of snow pants that the trio had worn on their excursion and shook them out. Matt knelt on the outside edge of the patio, a five-gallon planter in front of him.

"You're sure this will live?" he asked over his shoulder.

"I really don't know." Lauren, now mostly free of snow debris, moved to where he worked with a two-foot tall spruce. "Seems like it's worth a try though. Poor thing will die out there all unearthed like that."

They'd found a small slide zone on their hike, and at the edges of the trail of mud-streaked snow, the young tree had been tossed, root ball exposed, tips of feathered needles buried. She'd dropped to her knees in the snow, digging with her hands, and within moments, both Matt and Jackson were helping.

"What will you do with it?" Matt had asked.

Lauren had shrugged. "Your mom does plants, right? Flower arrangements? Maybe she could do a live mini-Christmas tree. Surely someone would like that."

Jackson had snorted. "Yeah, someone like Mom. Do you know how many trees she puts up at Christmas? Dad'll roll his eyes."

"And smile," Matt had said, a knowing expression on his face.

Anyone who had eyes could see Kevin Murphy adored his wife. And if they doubted the sincerity of the man's loving looks—and Lauren had no idea who would—they could just wander to the back of the house to find the expansive, gorgeous greenhouse he'd built for Helen's plant hobby.

Kevin loves Helen.

Lauren had chuckled as she fingered the engraving etched into one of the doorposts in the addition. A warmth flowed through her, imagining what thirty-five years of that kind of marriage would be like.

"We'll have to have Mom check the soil level." Matt packed black dirt around the thin trunk of the baby tree. "I never get it right." His grin found Lauren's eyes, and then he stood, his presence magnetic beside her. With a dip of his shoulder, he nudged her. "It was a good find. Mom will like it."

He'd not been wrong. Helen squealed and clapped her hands when she followed Matt's beckon to her workbench in the greenhouse.

"What's this?" she asked with delight.

"A live Christmas tree. Don't you start Christmas posts right after Thanksgiving?"

Helen's grin faded a touch. "Well, I have before, but my website..." She sighed. "I don't know. I'm just not good with that kind of thing. I've been thinking I'll just go back to selling in town at the open market on Saturdays."

"What?"

"The blog is so much work. I don't think I have it set up right—"

Lauren stepped closer. "You have a website and a blog?"

Helen sighed. "I sort of have a mess on the internet—not sure you could legitimately call it a website."

"Can I see?"

"Well, sure, but—"

"Mom, Lauren's really good with this kind of thing." Matt's large hands covered Lauren's shoulders, warming the chilled skin and making her heart move with pleasure. Though she knew she shouldn't swim in that delight, when she looked up to find his proud gaze on her, she sank in past her eyeballs.

Matt the Heartbroken...

The whisper faded even before the word *heartbroken* was completed, which made it easier to ignore.

"Matt, you can't volunteer someone's work for them."

"I'm volunteering myself." Lauren refocused on Helen, pretending as she spoke that she hadn't just turned to a pile of mush under Matt's touch and approval. "I'd be happy to look at it and help you if I can. If you'd like."

Helen's study was kind, even as her eyes moved from Lauren's face, up to Matt, still at Lauren's back, and back again. "I'd like that very much."

A fire crept up Lauren's neck, and she stepped from under Matt's hold. *What must she be thinking?* Possibly that Lauren was a mink, hunting for a man by winning over his mother. *I'm not hunting.*

She wasn't. Hadn't been.

We're friends. That had been the pact. We'd be friends.

That was still true.

And Matt is heartbroken.

Also still true.

"Come on, then." Helen snatched Lauren's hand, her kind smile and ways unchanged. "I'd love to see some magic."

Lauren followed, hand still swept up in Helen's. She glanced back at Matt, and he winked.

She told herself not to sigh. This weekend...

Might have been a mistake. Her heart might not recover.

***

Mornings were about the only time a hush could ever cradle the house, which had been the reason Matt had become a morning person. That, and the long-held desire of a boy wanting to be just like his dad.

For as long as he could remember, Matt had found his father in the tender dark hours of a day yet unborn, sitting in his leather chair, coffee cup full on the side table, Bible open in his lap. All through high school, Matt had mimicked this tradition silently given by his dad. Somewhere about age twenty-one, that habit had slipped.

But the predawn of that post-Thanksgiving morning found Matt in his spot. The place he'd claimed had been at the round table near a wide window facing east. There he sat, Bible open, mug seeping warmth into his palm, as the faintest hints of a new day streaked orange and pink beneath the tree-smattered horizon.

"Been a while since I've seen you here." Dad spoke softly from the opposite side of the room. "Missed the view."

"Me too," Matt said. Glancing over, he found his father's reading glasses slipped to the end of his nose, his attention on him rather than the Word. A narrow thread of shame slithered into the moment, though Matt knew Dad had not intended the comment to be a rebuke.

Folding his Bible closed, Dad stood, reached for his mug, and wandered over to Matt's table. "Where are you reading these days?"

"Isaiah."

"Yeah? The Evangelical Prophet. The Prince of Prophets..." Dad slipped onto the chair across the table. "Any reason you ended up there?"

Matt looked down to the thin leafs, running his finger over the printed *Isaiah* on the corner of the page. "Lauren had mentioned a verse in chapter forty. I thought I'd get some context."

Dad made a low humming sound of acknowledgment. "It's good to see you back at it."

"Yeah, it'd been a while." His stomach churned with the confession, and something unidentified turned in him as he reflected on why he'd taken up the morning reading habit again. When Lauren had challenged him about whether or not he was actually a Christian—though done mostly in good nature and as a reasonable check for her general safety—she had asked for his favorite verses. He'd been embarrassed to realize he only really had one in his bank—and it'd been from high school.

A growing Christian should have more stock in the Word than that. His dad sure did. And at one time, Matt had more invested and stored too. It was alarming how quickly those reserves had been lost. Ignored. As if it didn't matter to his everyday life.

Made him wonder at the time exactly how turned around he really was. He had a better view now, a few weeks into something of a recovery phase. He'd been a pretzel. Mind and heart twisted, confused, and turned around wrong.

"Your mom was thrilled with the work Lauren did on her website." Dad brought his mug to his lips, his steady focus on Matt.

Matt understood the underlying implications. Didn't feel confident enough to take them on straight though. "I'm glad. Lauren's good with that stuff."

"Seems to be." His mug clunked softly against the table. "Seems to be good for you, son."

"We're friends, Dad."

"Good place to start."

"Dad, I told you before I brought her here..."

He tipped his head, leaned in. "Matt, how about you tell me *why* you brought her here?"

That heat in his gut increased and soured, and he looked at his knuckles against the pages of God's Word. "She was going to stay at the lodge. I thought—"

"Think the kind of young woman she is, she would have been fine at the lodge with Harold and Emma—likely they would have appreciated her being there. Let's you and me be honest here."

Summoning some courage, Matt raised his gaze to meet his dad's. "I didn't want to risk running into Katrine on my own."

Nothing changed in Dad's expression as he tipped a slight nod. "And Lauren..."

"She knows that." An edge of self-defense made his voice crisp.

Shouldn't have. Dad was ever the gentleman and expected his sons to behave the same way. Though he'd been a kind and fun father, he also hadn't ever been the sort to shy away from a necessary confrontation with his young men.

"Have you let that one go?"

"Katrine?"

A silent dip of Dad's head confirmed it.

"I...think? I don't know, Dad. At this point, I don't even know what it was." No, that wasn't quite right. Matt rubbed his neck as his shoulders curled inward. "Maybe that's not true. Maybe I just don't want to say what it was."

"Think you need to?"

Matt inhaled, held the breath, and then surrendered. "It was...it was me telling God what I wanted. Insisting on my own way and being mad that He wasn't making it happen. It became an obsession. An idol." Emotion locked hard in his chest, and his fists curled into stiff balls.

Dad's hand, rough and worn but strong, covered those clenched fingers. "It's hard to face ourselves when we see failure."

Matt nodded, head still bowed.

Dad leaned back, the strength of his touch loosening and then falling away. "Do you know what I've been reading?"

"No," Matt said.

"Just today. Psalm Thirty-One verse nineteen. 'How great is your goodness that you have stored up for those who fear you.'" Dad moved forward again, this time leaning in enough to grip Matt's elbow. "Trust God's goodness, son. He is good. He means good for you, even when He tells you no. Even when His discipline feels hard. He is good."

Matt clapped a hand over the fingers that wrapped his elbow, and squeezed. "I know that, Dad. I'm seeing it now."

"Good." Dad bowed, as if lifting up a silent prayer. Likely he was. Likely, he'd been praying for Matt's eyes to be opened for many years.

Thank You for this good man—a godly father. Show me how to be more like him.

Dad stood, lifting his mug as he went. "For the record, Matt, I like Lauren. I like her a whole lot."

Then there was that—which was a problem. Because Matt did too.

He wished the things he'd clung to in the past didn't have a way of latching on to him now. He wished he'd have listened and trusted the goodness of God in the years before he and Lauren met. If he had, there probably wouldn't be a problem at all.

"Trust the Lord with all your heart, and do not lean on your own understanding." Dad moved to the sink, deposited his mug, and drifted into the shadows of the still-quiet kitchen. "God is good, son. Trust Him."

Chapter Fifteen
(in which Matt and Lauren get stuck)

"Connor left the house with two bouquets." Lauren snapped the seat belt buckle in place and sank into the heated leather seat. "Was he delivering for your mom?"

"No." Matt turned the engine and then looked at Lauren. "Those are from him—he pays Mom for them every year."

"Ah." Lauren's eyebrows shot up. In the four days she'd spent with the Murphy clan, she'd rather fallen in love...with all of them. The more withdrawn, quiet, and steady Connor had not been an exception. "Who's the lucky girl?"

"It's not like that." Matt's expression wrinkled, as if pained. "The flowers are for two families of a couple of classmates of his. It's kind of complicated and not something that he's known how to deal with."

"Oh." Lauren rolled her hands together. "I'm sorry."

"It's okay." Matt brushed the back of his knuckles across the hair that had curtained over her face. He'd been doing that more and more. Touching her. Folding her heart between thrill and caution.

After reversing out of the long, sloped Murphy driveway, he pointed his car toward town, which they'd drive through before they began the return journey to the lodge. The clouds ahead darkened with a heavy promise of more snow. Helen had sent them off with a warm thank-you to Lauren for all her help—

which delighted Lauren to no end—and a warning to Matt to drive cautiously.

I mean it, son. The reports say ice in the valley.

Matt had chuckled, hugged his mother, and told her goodbye.

Lauren had been sad to leave and relieved to be going. Matt had been... Oh goodness. Funny. Protective. Exactly like himself. Only better. Because his attention had pretty much been hers. All hers, as if that whole pretense of *come home with me as my shield against another woman* had dissipated completely.

And they both seemed to like it that way.

Which was not good.

Maybe it was? Perhaps Matt had intended to make her think and feel all the things he'd been making her think and feel. That he wasn't as brokenhearted over what's-her-name as he'd first thought. That Lauren hadn't been brought to distract and protect. That his heart might be still intact, and possibly even available...

"We need to fill up before we head over the mountain." Matt guided the car to a gas station. "Need anything?"

"Nope. Not after your mom's brunch and homemade mocha."

"Yeah, it's dangerous living in that house. She'll feed you. This is why all of us work hard—we'd be rolling around in life if we didn't."

Lauren could believe that. "Thinking of that mocha, I might sneak in to use the restroom."

"Gunner keeps the station clean. And Jackson's still at the house, so you should be good."

Matt winked. Lauren took it with a smile, the budding confidence in all those *maybes* growing strength.

As promised, the station had been clean, and Lauren whistled as she passed through the store on the way back out to the car.

"Have a good trip." The middle-aged man behind the counter gave her a small wave.

"Thanks." She knew her smile was too bright. Her step too light. Couldn't help it. The *maybes* just might bloom into real—

Three steps outside the door, Lauren froze. Nearly fell off the raised curb as her heart clenched hard. Across the way, just twenty feet in front of her, Matt grinned at Anne Hathaway. Well, she looked like Anne Hathaway, making Lauren feel like Plain Jane Pixie Pants.

"Lauren." Matt's voice stunned her out of the misery of her collapsing self-esteem.

"What?"

"You okay?"

"Yep." The snipped word set her in motion. Though wanting to liquify onto the wet pavement so she could slip down the storm drain, she straightened her shoulders and made her stride look as confident as...Anne Hathaway's.

Matt had finished filling the car and stood beside it, the Hathaway doppelganger smiling up at him as if he were Thor come down to earth, then briefly slid an unimpressed survey over Lauren.

"Who's this, Matthew?"

Matthew?

"Katrine, this is Lauren..."

A pair of perfectly plucked and lined brows lifted, as if both disapproving and curious. Mostly disapproving.

Lauren looked back at Matt. He seemed lost—maybe embarrassed?—as he watched Katrine's response.

"Lauren..." Katrine held an outstretched hand, as if one should kiss it.

Not gonna be me, and don't want it to be him. Lauren stepped forward, gripped the draping fingers, and gave them a squeeze. "Matlock."

"Yes. Lauren Matlock." Matt stood straighter. "Lauren and I work together. At a lodge. By the lake. You know, Tahoe. We met at the—well, anyway. We met. A few weeks back."

Lauren eyed him as if he'd lost his mind. Because she thought he'd lost his mind.

"I see." Katrine molded a pout onto her lips.

Disgust and irritation collided, creating a strong force of boldness in Lauren.

"Right. Matt*hew* here offered to let me spend Thanksgiving with his family." Lauren stepped away, pinning a glare on Matt. "Because he felt bad for me."

"What?" Matt whipped a look toward Lauren as she rounded the nose of the car.

"He's real nice like that." Lauren kept her eyes fixed on him. "Taking in orphans and rejects."

Now his expression morphed into confusion. "Wait. What?"

"Matthew is just the nicest of men," Katrine purred.

"Exactly. That's Matt Murphy. The nicest." Lauren opened her door, slipped into the car, and pulled it shut. Her heart thudded an angry staccato. Blood throbbed like lava through her veins. Mostly, she was mad at herself. She'd known. Not like Matt had made any big secret out of his feelings for Katrine.

She. Had. Known.

Goodness though. The man had turned into zombie Matt. Roll-over-like-a-dog Matt. Let-me-please-lick-your-boots Matt. Forget-Lauren's-last-name Matt.

Matthew Murphy may make me sick. How's that for alliteration, buddy? I could text it to your mom—

The pop of the driver's-side door startled her out of her fuming name game. Lauren eased a side glance, finding Matt gripping the steering wheel.

"You okay?" she asked, ice in her voice.

"Are you?" he nearly growled.

"What does that mean? *I'm* fine."

"That was..." His face turned to her. "What was that?"

"What was what?"

"I've never seen you be rude. To anyone. Ever."

"Oh." She sealed her lips. Held a hard stare. "Well, you only work with me. At the lodge. By the lake. So..."

Defeat slipped into his expression, while color brushed his cheeks. His gaze fell to the console between them, and then he shifted straight in his seat and started the engine.

Five minutes of shivering silence crept by as the car carried them down the highway. Space in which Lauren's ears rang while she replayed the whole scene in her mind like a broken record. Matt had been...

Unsure of what to do or say. That was what. He'd been awkward—and why did that surprise her? He'd been completely up front about why he'd wanted her with him—to help him face Katrine if the occasion arose. Arose it had, and Lauren had...

Been *so* ugly.

She inhaled, her breath shaky. Exhaled. Squeezed her eyes shut. And then looked at the silent, tense man beside her.

"I'm sorry."

His lips parted, and he glanced at her.

"I'm sorry I was rude and that I embarrassed you."

He winced. Sighed. Rubbed his forehead with his hand and then gripped the steering wheel with both fists. "I shouldn't have introduced you that way. I'm sorry."

Lauren swallowed, wishing away the urge to sob. "You'd told me why I was invited, so I shouldn't have been—"

"No, don't excuse me. I don't know why I'm that way with her. It's like a bad habit or something. I turn into... Man, I don't even know what."

On the next glance he shot at her, she saw torture in his eyes.

"She never wanted what was good for anyone but herself. Lauren, I left a promise to my Dad to work as his partner for her. Lived in an apartment that made me crazy, in a city I hated, at a job that made me feel like an idiot, all to impress a woman who..." His jaw clamped as he stared out the window.

The ice that had struck her heart cracked, and Lauren blinked. *A friend loves at all times.*

She'd promised to be his friend. That meant even when she witnessed his weaknesses. Even when it made her quiver with anger. With tentative motion, fingers shaking, she reached to cup his arm. Initially the muscles beneath her hand tensed, but then he sagged back against the seat.

"Who does that, Lauren?"

"A man who wants to see the best in another." She had no idea where that answer had come from, but she knew immediately it was true. At least, in this case, that was part of the story. Matt had an optimist's viewpoint. He saw the world and the people he encountered as good and full of possibility. Katrine had preyed on that, and Matt was only a man—open to manipulation and failure.

"That's generous of you," he said.

Not entirely. Because the statement was true, and also because inside she resented his blind attachment to Katrine and was still upset at the way he'd introduced them.

A fresh measure of quiet expanded between them as the road began to zig and then zag up the mountain. Though tempered by the idea of Matt having been played because of his good nature, the point simmered in Lauren's mind. He'd left behind everything for Katrine? Changed who he was to fit her ideal?

That was, well, nuts. Especially since Matt and Katrine had never been a real couple, and Katrine obviously didn't care about Matt's goodness or bring out the best in him.

"Why did you do all those things for a woman who never made a commitment to you?"

As Matt's lips pressed and his jaw tightened, Lauren agonized over her overstep. It really was none of her business.

Somehow though, it felt like her business, and that made this whole encounter miserable.

"I don't know." Matt's delayed answer came low.

The curves of the pass came and went, trees shuffling by in blurs of green smattered with white. The clouded sky above began to spit heavy white flakes, the snowfall wet and reducing visibility. As they neared the summit, Lauren was unsure if her roiling stomach was due to the motion of the car, the increasingly stormy conditions ahead, or the thick emotion that refused to settle in her gut.

Before he guided the car into the descent, Matt ran a hand over his head and gripped his neck. "You want the truth?"

Uh, did she? She wasn't sure.

"I think she became an addiction."

Guess she was going to get the truth whether she wanted it or not.

Matt plunged forward. "Like those games you'll never beat. There's always gonna be another challenge, another level with a new set of rules, and you'll never reach the end. Which is infuriating and stupid. But you just keep going back to it. You keep playing, knowing that you'll never really succeed. It becomes an addiction—but you won't admit it."

Wow. That was a pretty big admission. Lauren wrestled with equal parts pity and, honestly, judgment. A game, she got. Who hadn't got sucked into the vacuum of *Candy Crush*?

But with a relationship? How did that happen?

"You're disgusted, aren't you?"

"No." Lauren slammed away the uncharitable arrogance in her mind. "No, I'm not—I'm trying to understand. But I think that's a hard thing to admit."

He winced, and his knuckles turned white against the steering wheel. "Yeah," he whispered.

Another lull of edgy silence filled the car as they wove through the middle section of the pass. Lauren watched the road, hoping her stomach would settle soon. The last thing she wanted was to throw up on him. Again.

Matt's grip eased, and the tight muscles in his forearm and jaw loosened. "Tell me what you're thinking."

Catching her off guard, his request sounded almost like a plea. Uncertainty held her tongue.

"Please, Lauren. I want to know."

"I just wonder how that happened," she blurted, pressing a hand to her roiling middle. "How you got sucked in that far."

Though the shifting of his shoulders betrayed his discomfort, Matt nodded. "Me too. I keep going over it. Asking myself the same thing—how did I get that far gone?"

They eased out of the last curve and began the final downhill stretch that emptied into the charming mountain valley that had hosted Lauren's sweet daydream—one that she'd had to work not to dwell on the whole weekend. Strange, even now, with Matt's kryptonite exposed, her heart and mind still reached for that lovely ideal she'd imagined.

His sigh helped keep her in the present. "I want to blame it all on Katrine. She has a way of making people do what she wants."

"That's called manipulation, Matt."

"I know." He swallowed, then glanced at her. "I know, and my parents warned me about it. And that's the thing, I think."

"What?"

"I didn't listen because I didn't want to. I just wanted what I wanted, you know? With my parents—and so much worse, with God—I told them that the life I imagined with Katrine was good and was what I wanted. Didn't matter if my parents saw issues. Didn't matter if God was telling me it wasn't the best thing. I demanded." All the tension returned to his body, making his shoulders strain and his expression tight. "Have you ever done that? Told God that the thing you dreamed of was all you wanted and demanded that He make it happen—as if you knew better than He?"

As his voice caught and crimson crept up his neck, the vestiges of anger Lauren had entertained evaporated. Shame was a hard thing to shoulder. She wasn't in any position to mandate that he keep doing so. Not when she knew good and well that grace, though costly to Christ, was offered freely to all. Her. And him.

"No." He chuckled sadly. "No, I'm sure you'd never do that sort of thing."

Was that snide? Didn't sound malicious. But...

She held a long look on him, unsure of his comment, and he turned to look at her. And there they settled. The storm of her emotions and the intensity of his gaze—they both paused in that moment.

Which proved to be a mistake. At least the part of his gaze on hers, because one moment they were cruising safely toward the charming mountain village, veiled by the falling snow, and the next, the vehicle shifted momentum. The wheels fought for grip as power transferred from one side to another, but the black ice beneath them would not be navigated.

"Hold on." Matt held the steering wheel with one hand and

tucked her head into his shoulder with another as the car spun. Once. Twice.

And then jolted to a stop.

Matt's hold on her tightened as his car settled in a bank of plowed snow, rocking them left, then right. Forward, then back. He didn't let go even after the jerking motion stopped. Several warm breaths puffed into her hair, and as her heart hammered, fear-spiked adrenaline throbbing, she inhaled against him. Lemongrass and pine blended in her senses, adding something heady to the already mixed-up emotions crashing within.

"You okay?" he whispered, breath warm near her ear.

Lauren shook, and her stomach still threatened to empty, but she held fast—tucked deep in his protective hold.

"Yes," she responded, voice shaky.

"Thank You, Jesus," he whispered.

The staccato of his heartbeat throbbed through his shirt against her cheek, and for a moment, she clung to the imaginings that it was her, and not the accident, that had shot his pulse into a race.

Foolish. Think on things that are true.

Reluctantly, she pushed herself upright and his arm loosened. A chill hit her face as soon as she left his embrace, but instead of entertaining wishes and daydreams, she assessed their situation. The car had spun into a massive pile of snow—likely the doings of several road plows over the past weeks. Her side of the vehicle had pushed in deep, and a solid bank of snow blocked her exit. No doubt the passenger front end had been damaged. Maybe crushed by the tightly packed snow and ice.

Lauren looked back at Matt, who twisted his head left and then right, hand cupping the back of his neck.

"You're hurt," she said.

"Not bad."

"Whiplash?"

"Probably. I'll be okay." He turned his body to look back on the road behind them. "We'd probably better not stay here though. Roads that slick, there's a chance someone else could slide into us."

"Should we call the police?"

Matt took his phone from his console, held it up to eye level, and then lifted it farther. "No signal."

He didn't sound surprised.

"Do you think you can get us out of this bank?"

"Doubt it." He shifted into reverse. "But we'll give it a go."

The tires spun as he accelerated, the sound of rubber slipping against ice and slush telling.

Matt stopped, shifted into Park. "I have chains, but that's not going to do us any good if I can't move the vehicle to get them on."

"Now what?"

He looked at her, apology clear in his eyes. "Town's not too far." He pointed ahead. "I could go on my own, but I don't like the idea of you in here. Like I said..."

"Yeah. I don't want to stay." She reached into the back to gather their heavy coats, passed his over, and then crawled into the backseat.

"What are you doing?"

"Getting our boots out of the back."

He caught her heel. "I can walk around to get them."

"You're hurt."

"I told you—I'm fine."

She ignored him, leaned over the backseat, and shuffled through the luggage Matt had loaded that morning. When she located his heavy winter boots, she passed them forward and then retrieved her own pair. After warm gear had been applied, Matt slid out, and she followed him.

Cold snapped hard at her cheeks, and the falling snow peppered Matt's gray coat within minutes. She looked up to find his waiting gaze.

"I'm sorry, Lauren."

She looked back at the car, then down the road at the town. Putting aside the accident and the hard conversation that they'd had, she pushed a small grin onto her lips. "It's pretty."

"What?"

"This little valley and the town. I had thought it was pretty when we passed through before—the part I saw before I fell asleep. Now we get to see it up close."

A relieved—perhaps surprised—chuckle moved his chest, and then he pulled her into a side hug. Where she thought he'd put a teasing comment, likely ending with calling her Pixie Pants, he left a wordless space and then guided her down the road. As they walked, he kept a steady watch on the road, first ahead of them and then behind, clearly cautious.

"I'll tell your mom you're not nearly as reckless as she was afraid."

"She'll believe that." His arm slipped from her shoulders. "Especially after I plowed my car into a snowbank."

Not wanting him to feel bad, she latched on to his arm. He glanced at her with a half grin before he checked the road behind him again.

"There's a service station right there." She pointed to a log structure with a red tin roof.

"I see it." Matt pushed his hands into his coat pockets. "Are you sure you're okay?"

Lauren smiled full. "I'm sure."

"You were pretty shaky back there."

"Just adrenaline."

"Looked like you didn't feel so well even before I put us in the snow."

Oh. He'd noticed? "Just a little queasy."

"Car sick?"

She shrugged. "Maybe. The fresh air is helping."

They reached the edge of town, and Matt glanced backward again. "There's a truck heading this way. We'd better get across, I think."

Lauren nodded as he reached to grip her hand.

"Don't slip," he said.

"Good idea."

Easier said than done. The falling snow had turned the already icy roads into a glass-smooth rink. No wonder Matt's car couldn't find grip; there was none to be had. She and Matt slid across the road, wobbling for balance and at the same time pushing for speed. Lauren blew out a relieved breath when they safely reached the opposite shoulder before the truck came near to passing.

"Life with you is certainly an adventure," she said.

She couldn't read the expression in his eyes when he looked down at her, and regretted the easily misread comment. Unclasping his hand, she pushed forward for the building, wishing that somehow this day could be edited. No more awkward conversations. No more feeling...unstable.

Matt stayed at her side, his unusual quietness unnerving. When they reached the entry, he held the door for her and then headed straight to the service desk.

"Do you have a phone I can use?"

"Sure," answered the young man working behind the counter. "And we usually have cell service if you go up to the viewing deck." He pointed toward the loft, accessible by a set of wide log-hewed stairs.

"Thanks."

"You two need help?"

"Well." Matt cleared his throat. "Yes, actually. I hit some black ice, and now our car is buried in a plow drift." He pointed the direction they'd come from. "About a quarter mile that way."

The young man nodded, a hint of a smile on his face. "You're not the first. Sorry about that though." He turned to grab a card from a stack near the cash register. "My dad, he owns this place. He's got a truck that can get you out."

"That'd be great, but I think there's damage. Not sure the car will make it over the next pass."

He nodded. "He can tow you, but he won't do it until the weather clears. Likely, he won't even try to pull you out of the drift until after the roads are more solid."

"Probably smart. They're pretty bad."

"Good news though," the kid said. "It's warm and dry in here. We have pizza or sandwiches, if you're hungry. Hot cocoa in the machine." He pointed toward the soft drink station. "You're welcome to stay as long as you need. The loft is warm and has a good view. Just give my dad a call."

Chapter Sixteen
(in which Matt kisses Lauren)

What a perfect way to ruin a good weekend.

Matt sagged onto the wooden stool, facing the giant trapezoid window that lent a fantastic overlook of the river. If the past hour or two hadn't been a complete disaster, he would have smiled, appreciating the scene before him. Snow continued to fall in large flakes, quilting this picturesque valley with a peaceful beauty that clearly had a traitorous side.

Maybe a little like this friendship with Lauren.

As if making a fool of himself in front of her hadn't been bad enough. And man, that had been bad. He'd become a babbling idiot, all because Katrine had blindsided him with her...what? Her manipulative smile? Her well-practiced sultry pout? What was wrong with him that in a matter of heartbeats he'd become a complete idiot?

Charm is deceitful, beauty is vain...

Proverbs. That's where that one was from. Right next door to *a woman who fears the Lord is to be praised.*

He'd stood in the midst of both types a couple hours before and had become an idiot because of the first. Worse, he'd hurt Lauren's feelings, made her feel small in the doing of it.

When did I become this man?

That was the question. And as if all of that hadn't been bad enough, he'd managed to get them stuck in the middle of a snowstorm. Brilliant. Simply brilliant.

"Look at this." Lauren, carrying a cup of hot cocoa and a paper, slipped onto the stool next to his, no sign of distress in her voice.

Matt couldn't help staring at her, taking in the curve of her jaw, the shape of her nose, the way soft light gleamed off those loose coffee-colored curls. Couldn't keep his mind from the way she'd felt tucked up against him in the car, his hand lost in the thick mass of hair. All he'd been able to think, to pray, in those terrifying moments of spinning uncontrollably down the highway was, *God, protect her.*

"Hey." She tapped the paper she'd spread on the table in front of them. "Are you listening?"

"What? No. Sorry. I..."

"Do you see this ad?" She tapped again, and this time he focused on what she was talking about. "I think this place is right over there." Now she pointed out the window.

Matt read the first line: *Young tree farm for sale.* And then he looked up to follow the direction of Lauren's focus. There, behind the veil of falling snow, sat a small acreage with several rows of small evergreen trees.

"A Christmas tree farm?" he asked.

"Looks like it."

"It's got several years before it's worth anything, by the looks of it."

"What? Are you crazy?" Lauren gave him a playful shove. "Did you hear how much your mom sold that live Christmas tree for this morning?"

"No." Hadn't been paying too much attention because of all the whistling he'd been doing while he loaded the car.

"Nearly a hundred dollars, and I'm sure she could have gone much higher. It's a live tree, Matt. A live tree that can be planted..."

A grin broke on his mouth, which felt good. "So you're excited about this?"

"I think there's a lot of potential there."

"And you're the girl to tap it."

Her posture slumped. "Well, probably not."

Watching her excitement nose-dive jabbed pain into his chest. He moved closer, burrowed his hand into her hair to cup her neck. "I wasn't doubting it for a second, Lauren. You definitely could be the girl to make it happen. You did for my mom."

Wide, soft eyes latched on to him, and for a breathless moment, held. That pain near his heart softened and squeezed, but then she looked back at the table, moved from her stool and away from his touch.

His hand felt empty and cold. What was this need that had exploded in him recently? He couldn't stop himself from gripping her hand, grazing her face with his knuckles, feeling the warm softness of her hair...

"It's a cute place." A woman stepped up the last riser into the loft.

Together, they turned, startled.

"Sorry. I'm Marian Yost. My son is running the store downstairs, and you called my husband for a tow."

"Oh yes." Matt stepped forward, hand outstretched. "Thanks for letting us wait out the storm here."

Mrs. Yost nodded, then gestured toward the window. "You two should go check out the little farm. Needs a young couple to love it."

"We're not—"

"Do you know who owns it?" Matt spoke over Lauren's protest, not wanting to hear her say it. Say that they weren't together. Not a couple. Though he knew his head wasn't right yet—proven earlier that very day by his stumble in front of Katrine—and he knew these thoughts and feelings about Lauren were powerful all on their own and didn't need him to add fuel, he ignored the small voice of warning telling him to go cautiously lest he break something precious. Instead, he stepped beside Lauren, placing a hand on her back as if he had a right to do so.

Eyes wide, she looked up at him.

"Can't hurt to look." He dropped a wink.

"Exactly." The woman smiled. "It was my great aunt's. She

planted those trees about four years back, just seedlings then. Said she wasn't going to retire to a rocking chair and worked those acres diligently. Unfortunately, a heart attack took her at the end of this summer past."

"Oh, I'm so sorry," Lauren said.

"Thanks." She nodded, paused, and then nodded again. "She would have wanted someone with vision and enthusiasm to buy it. My husband and I have too much going on with this place. And my son has hopes for somewhere out of the valley. So the farm is for sale. But it's a good little acreage, and this town has a lot going for it, if you like small towns."

"Can we go look?" Matt couldn't tamp down his enthusiasm. Actually, he didn't even try.

"You bet." She waved them to follow as she headed back down the stairs. "I have a key to the house, if you want to peek inside. And feel free to wander the property. It reaches down to the river and over to the big stand of mature pines."

"Matt," Lauren whispered as he gripped her hand and led her down the steps.

"What's it going to hurt? We're stuck here anyway. Connor said he'd come take us the rest of the way to the lodge, but I told him not to leave until the weather and roads clear. What else are we going to do?"

She grabbed his arm and pulled him to a stop halfway down. "It's a false pretense."

Matt stopped, one riser below her, so their gazes were level. *What if it wasn't?*

Moving out of his grasp and down the stairs, Lauren spoke up first. "Mrs. Yost, thank you so much for the offer, but we aren't serious about this."

Down on the first floor by the office, the woman turned with a grin. "I appreciate your honesty. But really, dear, what's the harm in looking? You never know. You might just fall in love."

"Exactly," Matt whispered. At her sucked in breath and frantic backward glance, he grinned, though his own heart had lurched as well. *What's the harm?* Taking her hand again, he leaned toward her ear. "Just for fun. Play along."

This time, he kept his hold on her. While getting the keys from Mrs. Yost, over the bridge that spanned the gentle flow of steaming water framed with a crust of ice, until they reached the edge of the tree farm property, he held her hand.

Lauren had been stiff, her fingers rigid in his. But when he released her and she stepped in between a row of knee-high trees, her expression relaxed. Ungloving her hand, she held it out, palm down, brushing the tips of needles as she passed through the row. At the end, she turned to step down the next line of trees, and he caught joy on her face.

Matt trailed behind as she wove through the small farm, his heart delighting in her delight, his desire slipping further into his invention of them. When he motioned to the cottage, with a "Shall we see the view from inside?" Lauren lost all hesitation.

The house was small and simple. A tiny covered front porch—room for a bench and to store firewood to keep it dry. A narrow entry with enough space to set two pair of winter boots, neatly lined up—his and hers. A clean eat-in kitchen. A cozy living area, sans a television but complete with a woodburning stove and a small French door leading to the back. A picture window there beside that French door gave a view to the rows of trees and the river below.

Lauren stopped there in her stockinged feet, her coat half unzipped and her hat freckled with melting snowflakes. Her cheeks, rosy from the cold, lifted as she scanned the view outside. Matt stood beside her, enchanted.

"Such a view," she said. "A lifetime wouldn't be enough."

No. It wouldn't.

The line between real and pretend blurred into nonexistence. Matt slid nearer, lifting an ungloved hand. His fingers grazed the plane of her chin, lifting her face until her eyes found his. She didn't move or flinch, only watched while the pad of his thumb drifted over the soft rose of her cheekbone. He lifted his other hand to trace the wave of her hair, tucking a lock behind one ear. With the cup of his palm, he cradled her head. Pulse throbbing, mouth tingling with desire, he leaned to brush his lips across the arch of her eyebrow.

A soft sigh lifted her breath to his neck, feathering him with warmth, fueling the longing to taste her mouth.

Ah, but this moment was one to savor. As he brushed a slow, gentle kiss to her temple, her hands pressed against his chest. His mouth drifted to the smile lines near her closed eye, the bridge of her nose, her cheekbone. Her fingers curled into the fabric of his flannel, exposed by his open coat, and her chin tipped up. When finally his lips found hers—soft, warm, and willing—a groan of relief rumbled from his throat. His tentative kiss gave way to more as her lips parted to him.

This, Lord!

The thought was a hallelujah and a query all at once. And it seemed, as Lauren folded against him, that heaven responded with an *amen*. His thoughts melted into the thrill of this pleasure.

Until her palms flattened, back stiffened, mouth pulled away. *No! Not enough.*

Though wanting only to taste those sweet lips again, Matt fought through the haze of yearning to look at her. She stared at him, confusion and hurt in those beautiful dark eyes.

She said nothing.

His pulse throbbed into the strain of silent questions between them. Stepping backward, her hands slipped from his chest, leaving him bereft of her touch.

He watched her, bewildered.

"Lauren," she said, voice strained.

"What?" he whispered.

She pressed her hand to her chest and then shuddered. "I'm Lauren."

What did she think? That he'd not known the woman he'd kissed? "I'm aware, Pixie Pants." When he lifted a small grin, reaching for her again, she shook her head and retreated another step.

"I'm not going to be your rebound, Matt." She blinked, then moved away. The floor creaked under her footsteps. He heard her

sniff as she stopped in the entry to step into her boots.
Go! Make it right. Tell her...
What? That he...he...what?
Don't mess with Lauren.

With one hand, he gripped the hat on his head as Mr. Appleton's firm warning echoed in his mind. The other clutched at his chest.

Where there had been the warmth of her, there was now the chill of emptiness. In the place of joy and longing, a crushing rejection. Worse, an aching knowledge that this thing he'd done, this game he'd played...

What could be the harm, he'd asked?

His heart. And hers. Now bruised. Maybe broken. And his mind too much in a jumble to think how to make it right.

***

The muscles in her face ached with the effort it had taken to maintain a fake smile. All through lunch—kindly offered by Mrs. Yost—through the socially acceptable small talk during which she'd hoped desperately she didn't look as miserable as she felt.

Though she'd sensed Matt's gaze on her more than once, and his nearness drifted close several times, she couldn't bring herself to look at him and definitely couldn't handle the thought of his touch. She'd been exposed, completely undone as she'd lost herself in his kisses. How could she go back to being his friend now?

Honestly, she didn't think she could. Not with the humiliation she felt at being found out, and the rising resentment that Matt would use her like that.

Had she misread him that badly? She thought him a good man. Heartbroken, and a bit lost because of a stupid, heartless woman who cared for no one but herself. But overall, she believed his heart to be kind.

That had not been kindness. That had been Matt taking what would cost him nothing. Her heart without the benefit of his.

So stupid, Lauren.

Now what?

Relief had crashed over her when Mrs. Yost presented her with a soft, heavy blanket and an invitation to rest in the office. There she'd found a short sofa, just long enough for her if she curled into a ball. All the better, as it seemed that way she could protect her battered heart. Matt had stolen into the room as she settled against the cushions, and he attempted to tuck the blanket around her.

"Don't," she spoke low.

"Lauren—" He moved her chin, forcing her to finally look at him.

"Please don't, Matt." Her plea came softer and seemed to pierce him, as his expression crumbled.

"Lauren, I didn't mean to hurt you. I—"

Unable to withstand his misery alongside her own, Lauren moved her chin from his hold and looked to the blanket. "I know." She inhaled, clamped her jaw, worked for control. "We'll be okay, Matt."

"What does that mean?"

She blinked and then forced herself to meet his gaze again. "We just got lost in a game. We were both stupid. I'll get over it."

"But—"

"We promised, right? Friends. That was the deal."

She couldn't say how he took that. He didn't say anything, and she'd lost the willpower to hold his eyes.

The afternoon wore on. She pretended to sleep. Then read a few magazines. Finally, Connor arrived. They crammed into his pickup, Lauren snug in between two large Murphy men. She kept quiet, answering only direct questions. By the time they reached the lodge, well after dark, she truly was exhausted.

Connor caught her while Matt took her luggage upstairs, hand on her shoulder and worry written on his face. "What'd he do?"

"I'm sorry?"

"My brother." He folded his arms over his chest. "He might be taller than me, but I can take him."

She breathed a halfhearted laugh. "Thanks, Connor. But we're fine."

"Not according to that long drive full of tense silence."

"I'm just tired."

He watched her, giving her one slow headshake. "Can I tell you something, Lauren?"

"Okay."

"Some things don't get fixed by ignoring them. And it can be too late to try when we finally realize it."

She studied him. "That sounds like a lesson coming from a man who knows."

"I do." He squeezed her arm. "Trust me when I tell you that you don't want to learn it the way I have."

"Okay." Someday maybe she'd have the courage to ask him more. That night, though, everything seemed like too much.

His hand still rested on her arm. "And for the record, Matt's a good man. Sometimes he's stupid, but that just genetic. All men seem to have it."

Despite her emotional wear, Lauren laughed and then hugged him. "Good night, Connor. Thanks for rescuing us."

Connor squeezed her shoulders and spoke lightly. "I'm on your side, Lauren. Whatever he did. Just so you know."

"Thanks." She wished it helped.

***

"What happened?"

Matt pretended he didn't hear his brother's question as he filled up the gas tank.

"Matt."

Ugh. That commanding voice. It grated. Especially since Connor had firm charge of it long before he'd ever entered the military at all.

"I just messed up, okay?" Matt jammed the lever back into the pump and turned to crank the gas cap back in place. "We'll figure it out though."

"She's pretty upset."

"I know."

"Women like her don't get that upset unless their heart is involved."

"What do you know about it?" Matt caught up to the words that had flown out of his mouth about a half second after it was too late.

Connor flinched but didn't back down. "I know enough to know what I'm talking about."

Matt looked at his feet. Nodded. "Yeah. I'm sorry."

"Look. I have to live with the things I did. *Forever*, Matt. Do you get that? I don't get to apologize—to either of them."

Inside, Matt shook with emotion for Connor. It was a heavy burden to carry. Too heavy, and everything in him wished for respite for his younger brother. Connor had been young and ignorant when all of it had happened.

"Don't let things go unsaid," Connor whispered. "You might not get tomorrow. That's all I'm saying."

Chapter Seventeen
(in which Lauren struggles with headaches)

The pain behind her eyes would not be quelled. Not for Tylenol or Advil, for oils or for caffeine. For three days it throbbed, a dull ache that stole her energy and made working on the screen a nauseating chore.

Lauren guessed that the relentless headache stemmed from a lack of consistent sleep—and that, from being upset. Chiefly with herself—because she could not delete the replay of her and Matt's kiss any more than she could convince her heart that going back to the friends pact they'd made wouldn't be that painful. But also, her unsettled spirit was due to Ashley's change in tone in the texts they'd exchanged.

The most recent, a humble beg for Lauren to go back east for Christmas.

I feel like you're leaving us, sis. Not just in geography, but in heart. Please come home for Christmas.

Lauren wavered in the uncertainty of what to think or do with such a convincingly sincere plea. She hadn't planned to fly back for the holidays. Finances weren't yet that stable to afford a trip, and the winter season at the lodge was proving to be a busy one—a cheerful revelation, as she'd worked hard on marketing and booking. Even with Mr. Appleton's insistent rule about not working on the holiday, traveling across the continent seemed too far a stretch for one or two days off.

But the real rub? Lauren wasn't sure she was ready to go back. There were places in her heart concerning both Ashley and her dad that were, as yet, unresolved.

"Morning, Lauren." Matt rumbled softly above her.

He'd seemed entirely absorbed in his morning Bible reading while she'd doctored her coffee, turned on the computer, and leaned into her cupped hand to massage the ache at her temples.

"Headache still?" he asked, his voice threaded with concern.

"Yes." She made herself sit up. "I'll be okay though."

He studied her with a folded brow, as he had several times the past few days. Hesitation and regret became a veneer over his normally playful and confident expressions. "Can I do anything to help?"

She looked at her work screen, not liking the spike that had been driven into her chest back in the valley and twisted every time she witnessed his discomfort with her. If she could just forget. Just find a way to accept the original terms of this relationship. Then they'd be okay. They'd both be all right.

Yeah. Just...if.

"I took some Tylenol," she said, trying to sound positive. "Hopefully with that and the coffee, the ache will ease soon."

"Are you drinking enough water?"

Lauren wasn't sure if it was the mildly condescending question, the gentle tone hemmed with worry, or her general crabbiness that spiked her irritation. But climb it did. "Yes, Dr. Matt*hew*. I'm drinking water." She lifted her chin. "I'm also eating sufficiently and getting in my morning walk. Thus, it's just a headache. It'll go away. Eventually."

Though he flinched, Matt didn't duck at her snark. "That fire makes your eyes darker."

"What?"

"When you get mad or you're passionate about something, the brown of your eyes deepens. Gets darker."

How often had he observed that?

Never mind. She didn't want to know. Too late, she tried to override her curiosity with indifference, and a sharp ache jabbed in her chest.

Matt laid an arm on the counter and leaned over into her work zone. "What can I help you with today?"

At his kind tone, her heart squeezed. Shouldn't have. This wasn't new—he'd asked this very question most mornings since they'd both started at the lodge. Once they'd figured out the run of the place and had agreed that they needed to find ways to boost the lodge's profit margin for Mr. Appleton—which had pretty much been immediately—this interchange had become a pattern. Matt managed the maintenance and activities of the lodge—and he did it with the kind of care and attention one would expect from someone who had skin in the game, not merely an employee. Lauren attended to the management details—marketing, booking, and guest services. Both, along with Emma, saw to the housekeeping chores, which changed from day to day depending on guest counts, checkouts, and Emma's kitchen-duty load.

Thus, this daily query from Matt was not a recent development. He asked out of habit and care for his job. Not for Lauren—not for any kind of relationship platform.

For work only.

Ah, but the low rumble of his voice, the way he leaned in, keeping that steady gaze on her...

Stop it. This isn't helping either of you move forward.

Under pretense of looking at the daily notes sent out by Mr. Appleton and Emma, Lauren clicked several times on the screen. She didn't need to look—she'd done so already—but she needed a moment to gather herself.

"The Driftwood room needs the mattress flipped, and the family staying in the cabin said there was a rattling noise when the heater kicked on last night. Also, Mr. Appleton noted that the woodpile up at the house looked about half used." She looked up.

Matt nodded. "I saw that yesterday. I'll get on it this afternoon, after I see to the other things." He paused. "Anything else?"

Why did he have to stare in that penetrating way, as if he wanted an answer that had nothing to do with work? Back to the computer screen. She cleared her throat. "Looks like we have six snowshoers today, and a pair for cross-country skiing."

A beat slogged by, woven with a sense of...disappointment? Then, "Got it." He hovered, waiting for...

What?

She raised her gaze to him.

"Will you feed the horses with me this afternoon?"

Such an innocent question shouldn't make her heart pinch. Not like she hadn't fed the animals with him before. Many times. Just not since Thanksgiving. She ducked away again, lest he read her confusion—or rather, her longing for things that were beyond their reach.

"We'll see," she mumbled.

His answer came only in silence, and then he moved away. Glimpsing his back as he exited the front door, it seemed his shoulders slumped.

***

That persistent headache of Lauren's nagged him.

Matt measured the horse's grain, wishing to hear the soothing sound of Lauren's quiet chatter to the animals as he prepared their feed. Every day for the past week he'd missed her, and not just at feeding time. He missed her easy conversation. The way he felt entirely himself—but in the best way—in her presence. Missed the way their banter made him feel light. And the way she could quote verses in a conversation as if the Word of God sprouted naturally from the warm soil of her heart, gently challenging him to sow the same seeds in his own life.

In the week since the accident in the valley—since the day he'd messed everything up—Lauren had kept herself in reserve. Held away from him with careful precision. Matt knew they needed to have a real conversation to clear the mixed-up things between them. He had taken Connor's warning seriously—his brother knew what he'd spoken about. But this unending headache that had plagued her...

How could he expect to dive into the deep and murky places he'd carved into their relationship when he knew she was in pain, not to mention certainly exhausted?

Little help here, God?

He lifted the plea as the sound of a car engine hummed from the front side of the lodge. The Hemfords probably. The only guests remaining on the property this morning—and they had plans to head to the downhill slopes for the afternoon, joining the other two families staying at the Lake Shore Lodge for the week. Likely that was them leaving for the day.

That left the resort empty for the next few hours. Maybe his opportunity? He'd worked double-time that morning to get his work for the day shored up and had made sure that the rooms, cabin, and house had been stocked with freshly laundered towels and any requested toiletries, and he had taken on the cleaning chores for the house, all in hopes that Lauren's afternoon would be clear.

She could use the rest, and he was going to do everything he could to see that she got it.

This tenderness he felt toward her—jointed tightly with a protectiveness unparalleled by anything he'd experienced before—had risen strong and fierce. Oddly, it had only grown in the days of distance between them. More so than anything he'd experienced when it had come to Katrine. With her, the push of his emotions had been to gain her attention, to show her he was the best man. It had been selfish. Though last week he'd claimed to Lauren that Katrine had been a person only concerned with herself, he'd come to realize that his drive hadn't been much different. He'd wanted what he wanted for himself, for his satisfaction.

Love given for selfish gain is not love at all. To love is to know the cost to oneself with a willingness to, even if that price be everything, give it for the good of the other. Jesus said there is no greater love than this, that one lay down his life for another. This is the ultimate standard of love.

Words scrawled out on a lined page with a shaky hand. Matt's own, to his astonishment. Penned the night before last as he'd read over John's account. A boldness stirred in his inner being even while conviction had pierced, feeling somehow like a sense of true manliness, taking on muscle and power.

He had claimed love for Katrine. It had not been so. Not by the standards of heaven.

God's firm *no* to him on that account had been for good. For both himself and for Katrine. For the first time in months, Matt's heart turned with real gratitude where that issue was concerned. Here was proof—he could trust the goodness of God's heart, even if it felt harsh in Matt's moments of blindness.

Grain poured into the feed bunk, and Matt ran his hand along the thick winter coat beneath the mare's mane. As soft fur met his palm, he grinned, and Sheela nickered between snuffling her treat. The air felt clean in the mild chill of that sunny afternoon. Shutting his eyes, he summoned again the image of those words on a page tucked into his Bible upstairs.

And what of Lauren?

Though things between them were unsettled, he felt a solidness hold him fast. He missed her smile. More, though, he wanted her best. Truly and honestly, that was his heart for her. For the moment, it seemed the good he sought would be relief for her headache. For rest.

So yes, with prayer and effort, he was going to find a way to make that happen.

And tomorrow? He'd look for another way to bring her good.

***

Matt had done the bulk of her work. At least, the work of housekeeping. And then he'd come in at lunch, wearing that genuine concern he'd donned of late, asking her to lunch. They often ate together as a practice of convenience. But he had asked her to eat with him specifically, rather than a general *ready for some grub?* She braced herself for the kind of conversation that seemed overdue. Hard and honest, in which he would say he hadn't meant to kiss her, and please would she forgive him and let it go? The one she dreaded because she didn't want to hear him say he didn't mean it and wanted her to forget it.

She couldn't let it go. Mind and heart had refused to forget. She hadn't accomplished the release over the days since and didn't feel any nearer to doing so that afternoon.

So reluctantly she went to lunch, not hungry and feeling even more wound up and sick about the pending conversation, only to find he didn't bring it up. Instead, he'd asked if she was caught up with her computer work.

"Yes, for the most part," she answered.

"So you could get a nap?"

She blinked. Was he being condescending again? Her stare must have communicated something suspicious to him.

"I'm just worried about you, Pixie Pants."

The use of his nickname for her smoothed many rumpled feathers, and in the next moment, she found herself near to tears. And what was that all about? When had she become a weeping willow?

His fingers traced the curtain of her hair, tucking one side back. "You're so tired, and seems like maybe you're coming down with something."

"Yeah," she breathed, blinking back the stupid moisture that flooded her eyes.

"Go sleep then." He sat back, taking away his touch. Leaving her with a large helping of longing.

How pathetic of her was it she wished for the comfort of those work-worn fingers? Shutting her eyes, she sorted her jumbled thoughts, fought past her surging emotions, looking for her reserve of self-control.

"Lauren, I can take care of the lodge. Should be quiet for a few hours anyway. I'll text you if there's something I can't handle."

Ah... The squeeze within her chest pulsed with warm ache. Why did he have to be so nice? It'd be so much easier to let go of this crush she'd developed if he didn't insist on being so...

"Go on, Lauren." His hand cupped her elbow, and then she was being escorted out of the kitchen, her feet moving as if separate from her command.

She stopped in the hall and found the discipline to look up at him. There he stood watching her with unveiled tenderness. *Matthew Murphy might make me cry.*

His hand lifted again, this time to brush her temple with his thumb. "See if you can't finally get rid of this, hmm?"

That would be lovely. This headache had stretched on excessively long. But lovelier still? To be folded in his arms. To feel the solid thud of his heart against her cheek. To think that there existed more than a wispy daydream that the fondness of his affections had shifted to her.

She turned away on the unhelpfulness of that thought, leaving the comfort of his touch, and took herself up the stairs. *God, I think I love him. Help me to feel right about him. To do what is right.*

After several moments of tears, the flow of which she finally lost the will to fight against, she slept.

Chapter Eighteen
(in which Matt takes Lauren snowshoeing)

She awoke with only a trace of what had been an ongoing throb. For reasons she couldn't identify, the rest she found had finally been deep, sweet. Even though the grit in the corners of her eyes reminded her of how she'd fallen asleep, she felt renewed. Ready to face Matt again.

Maybe ready to begin again.

That seemed odd, but she chose gratitude for the sense of renewal, rather than rummaging through questions that only confused, only frustrated.

The afternoon slipped by uneventfully, and in the evening, Matt refreshed the fire as he always did, then settled in that chair she now thought of as his, with a copy of a Grisham novel. When for the past several days she'd retreated to her tiny apartment, hoping to find real rest—and if she was being honest, avoiding him—she instead gripped a copy of *Magnolia Market* in her hand and sat on the sofa across from the fire.

Matt glanced up from his book, held a look for two heartbeats as his expression eased into something gentle. "Head okay?"

"Much better. Thanks for letting me rest this afternoon."

Light touched his eyes, and he held her gaze. At last the final traces of his concern, worn for too long, dissipated completely.

"I'm glad," he said, his voice low and soft.

She determined their friendship had found firm footing again. And that was enough.

***

Lauren buried her nose in the soft cradle of the mare's neck. "I've missed you. Did you miss me?"

Matt's chuckle drifted from the other side of the animal, where he forked grass hay into the bunk. "She asked about you every day."

"I'm sure." She glanced over the animal's head, a playful smile on her mouth.

Matt met her look. "The guests are skiing again today. We could take them out with the sleigh."

Tempting. She hadn't been out on the ride yet. But she knew Emma was hard at work, preparing a larger meal than usual for the group's last evening at the lodge. "Sleigh rides usually take a couple hours. I don't think I should be gone that long."

The sound from Matt's throat was either a grunt or a sigh, she wasn't sure which. He leaned the pitchfork against the side of the bunk and then rested his arms over the back of the horse. "How about a hike? I went up to the ridge-point view a few evenings back. It's quite a sight and only takes about twenty minutes to reach."

She'd heard several guests rave about the view from the ridge and had thought several mornings that she should go see it on her walk. But she hadn't been sure of the trail and wasn't quite adventurous enough to try to find it on her own.

"We could take our lunch with us, if you're worried about time." Something in Matt's voice hinted toward a plea.

Perhaps that conversation she'd been dreading weighed against him and this was how he wanted to have it. Probably for the best. Though she felt better about the re-footing of their friendship, it'd be good to clear the air completely. She'd tell him it was okay. She'd forget that kiss he hadn't meant—she'd get over it. She'd determined their friendship was the important kind, the kind worth the work required to forgive and to mend.

She'd not tell him she thought herself in love. For so many reasons, that bit of truth would only complicate things more. Chiefly, because Matt wasn't ready for it, and though she very much wanted him to find stability, she didn't want to be his post-Katrine recovery plan—at least not in a way that would end up breaking her heart.

Perhaps that was selfish—she wasn't sure.

"Lauren?"

"Yes." Realizing that her attention had drifted from him back to the horse as she wove through her thoughts, Lauren returned her focus to Matt. "Yes, a hike sounds like a good idea. I've wanted to see the ridge."

His grin looked evermore like old Matt—lighthearted and comfortable. "I'll get the snowshoes ready then."

She nodded. "I can grab some sandwiches."

He stepped backward, retrieving the fork. "I'll see you in a few minutes?"

She agreed, and they parted only to reunite at the equipment barn. Matt presented her with the aluminum snowshoes, a wide contraption of shiny tin, dark polyethene decks, and hard plastic ratchet straps. He fitted her boots and gave her the rundown on walking with the contraptions.

"The trail is pretty well laid out, so it's gonna be more like walking than you think. On the climbs, just trust your crampons—for the most part, the trail is packed in, so you won't have to do that work." Matt finished locking down her heel straps and grinned up at her. "You'll love it, Pixie Pants."

Shifting the poles he'd handed her so that one was in each mitted hand, she nodded. "Okay then. Let's get going so you can laugh when I fall on my face."

"I'd never do that."

"Right."

"Maybe a small chuckle. But not a full-out laugh. I'm not mean—usually. And I'd help you up."

He nodded ahead, and she started toward the general trailhead that would lead them toward the public lands and to the trail that would cut east toward the ridge that served as Lake Shore Lodge's stunning backdrop.

"I trust you for that." She nudged him as she passed, and the weight of his shoulder pushed into her in response.

The walking path cutting through the snow was wide enough for side-by-side travel until they reached the cutoff where several trails diverged. In a few places, she saw smaller, less established trails that meandered through the woods.

"Are these yours?" she asked, nodding at one of the wandering snowshoe prints.

"Yeah. My firewood forays."

Thinking about the day she'd helped him with that chore made a surge of warm yearning rush through her. Things between them had been simpler then, as they'd just embarked on a promising new friendship while simultaneously stepping into new jobs together. Even then, though, when he'd shared more about Katrine, there had been something within her that had pushed against that part of his life. A resentment where there should have been more compassion. Though she wouldn't have owned it then, now she could recognize that resentment had been the early stages of jealousy.

Something she wrestled with big time now.

Shortly after taking the cutoff, their assent began, and Matt took the lead. Lauren struggled for a while, leaning too far into the hill and often having the front of her snowshoes dig into the snowpack when she tried stepping forward. More than once, she fell forward, catching herself with the poles most times. Once, though, she misplaced even that and landed forward and to the side, off the trail.

Matt turned, a good-natured chuckle rumbling from him as he bent to help her back onto her feet.

"Trust the crampons, Lauren. You're working too hard."

"I'm not even sure what you're talking about."

He lifted a foot, crossed it over one bent leg, and pointed to a set of small claws fitted under the deck where the toe of his boot rested. "These. They'll do the digging in for you, especially since this trail is already packed for us. But if you don't trust them to do what they're intended, you'll end up working too hard, at best—or taking a spill."

She took his hand, and he pulled her out of the three feet of loose powder that had sucked her into its depths. Once he had her steady on her feet, he reached around her to brush the powder from her shoulder, arm, hip, and then head.

It took an intentional talking to herself not to imagine his movements as tender, his nearness as anything resembling a hug. He'd do such for anyone. Her. A guest. Katrine...

Don't go there.

He stepped away, somehow magically not getting the tail of his long snowshoe caught in as he moved. "Ready to go again?"

Nodding, she side-shuffled back to the trail and then followed up as they returned to the hike. Though she had to make a mental effort to *trust the crampon*, as she did so, she discovered Matt had been right. Her strides settled into something of a rhythm that didn't require nearly as much effort as she'd been putting in before, and as she gained the feeling of this new activity, she found herself breathing easier. Trusting her equipment. And enjoying the view.

To her left, when the trees allowed a peek of the lake, she found glimpses of the vast ice-edged waters extending beyond the smaller cove that served as the lodge's front-yard view. Snow-laden evergreens mingled with leafless skeletons of trees that had been bronze, red, and gold months before. On this nearly windless day, the free waters of the lake rested in a placid peace, becoming a mirror for the cloud-dusted pastel-blue sky.

The ridge came into view—marked by a rustic arbor and bench made of cedar and black oak. A clearing of thirty feet surrounded the visitors' point, allowing for a vista of the lake to the southeast and the rising folds of the Sierras to the north and west.

The bench rested in the afternoon sun, slightly shaded by the artistic crossbars of the cedar arbor, but free for at least another hour from the shade delivered by the surrounding evergreens.

Matt made his trail directly to it, and Lauren followed, a smile lifting not only her mouth but everything within her.

"It's breathtaking," she said.

Matt turned but didn't sit. Instead, he scanned the horizon, taking in the scene as if for the first time. Captivated wonder lit his eyes. He'd been up here more than once, and Lauren knew it. Familiarity had not robbed Matt of appreciation, and his wonder had seemed to turn to a silent form of worship. How could she not love that?

"It is something, isn't it?" He nudged her arm. "Give me a verse for it."

Lauren stood wordless. Spellbound by the enormous beauty surrounding her, unfolding before her. And caught once again by the man who didn't mean to snare her affection.

"Come on now, Lauren." His soft rumble, the feathery way he spoke her name, made her want to sigh. "I know you've got a verse tucked into that heart of yours."

"Hmm..." She shut her eyes, searching within, surrendering to the loveliness of the moment, and rather than turning it all inside out and upside down, she lifted the emotion up to God. "The heavens declare the glory of God; the skies proclaim the work of His hands. Day to day they pour forth speech; night after night they reveal knowledge. They have no speech; they use no words; no sound is heard from them. Yet their voice goes out into all the earth, their words to the ends of the world."

Matt held his place, humming his acknowledgment. Then, "Where is that found?"

"Psalm Nineteen."

She peeked at him, and he looked down at her. In the next few heartbeats, his study turned warmer, somehow more intimate. Melting her heart, mixing her up all over again.

"You amaze me, Lauren—make me want to be more. Better."

Ah, the ache. It burned as it spread, a delicious pain that would surely turn to regret. She swallowed, cleared her throat, and turned her attention back to the beauty that spread all around them. "It's the Word of God, Matt. Not me."

Though his steady gaze beckoned, she did not comply, as the compression near her lungs made drawing breath difficult. Then his gloved hand found hers, squeezed, and fell away as he turned toward the bench behind them.

Matt sat, slipping the pack he'd carried from his shoulders. After unzipping it, he tugged out two sandwich bags. "Peanut butter and jelly?"

"Not from Emma's kitchen." Lauren forced a laugh as she lowered onto the spot beside him, determined to let those breathless moments dissolve. "I think this is turkey and cranberry salad on wheat."

"Mmm..." Matt ripped into the food like a starved man, apparently unaffected by what had passed between them. "My mom makes something like this with holiday leftovers."

Sounded like Helen. Lauren took her time with her portion, eyes straying more to the lake below than to her food. For several long, settled moments, they sat quietly, savoring the view, the simple food, and what she was determined to return to—easy company.

"I'm glad you're feeling better," Matt said. Something in his voice seemed wary. As if this was a lead in to a tenuous conversation.

So it would be. Lauren braced her emotions. Prepared to bury further what she really felt. "Me too."

The forest whispered and cracked as trees danced with the gentle stirring of life and snapped under the heavy burden of snow. A chattering chased up the hill—likely that of squirrels—and every few breaths, a bird sent its song onto the clear afternoon air.

"Mom says to tell you you're welcome to come back for Christmas."

So many ways to take that hesitant statement. His mom's invitation—not Matt's. The tentative nature of his offer—because he wasn't sure it would be welcomed, or because he wasn't sure he wanted to extend it? Did he realize how much he continued to muddy her heart?

Lauren sighed but brushed on a smile, as if that could hide her true reaction. "Tell her thanks. But I'm going back east."

"You are?" No covering his surprise there.

"Yes."

She again felt his look upon her but avoided meeting his stare.

"When did you decide that?"

"Recently." As in that morning. She'd gone to talk to Mr. Appleton about taking the full week off. He'd agreed without hesitation, kindly encouraging the visit with her family.

"You—" He shifted beside her, the movement stiff. "You didn't say anything before."

"I had thought to stay at the lodge before, to celebrate with Emma and Harold. But Ashley has asked me to come back, and I need to go."

Matt became a statue at her side. She couldn't even make out the sound of his breath, though he sat nearly shoulder to shoulder with her. Unable to avoid him any longer, Lauren turned to him. He stared out over the distant lake, the wonder that had painted joy and light on his expression now dim. The concern he'd worn throughout the week had returned, folding his brow, pressing a need within her to ease his worry.

"I ran from something that perhaps I should have dealt with, Matt." She couldn't make her voice much more than a whisper. "I need to go back, to see what is salvageable with my sister."

The turn of his chin toward her came slow, and with it, the depths of his searching eyes. "Are you running now?"

It seemed an unfair question, and she flinched. "I think you and I both have some things to figure out. On our own."

"Because of what happened at Thanksgiving?"

She looked away. Nodded.

"I'm sorry, Lauren." The weight of his body invaded her space as he anchored an arm on the bench behind her. "So sorry that I messed up that day."

There it was. The thing she hadn't wanted to hear. That he hadn't meant it—it had been a foolish mistake and he wished it back. Unable to banish the emotion his apology provoked, she swallowed.

"I know," she whispered. "And it's"—she cleared her throat—"it's okay, Matt."

Please let that be true. Someday. Please let it be okay. Let Matt and me be okay. As much as he made her ache, she was certain that banishing him from her world would be much worse.

She looked toward the lake, the beauty there still captivating, but the moment had turned hard all over again. Matt pulled back from her space, then leaned forward, pressing elbows into knees.

A long span of struggling silence whispered between them.

"You're coming back, right?"

Lauren forced her eyes back to him, finding his gaze already locked on her. "Yes." She found the will to lift the corners of her mouth. "It's just for Christmas. I'll be back."

He examined her, and she dreaded that he might find the truth. By the tightening of the corners of his eyes, she feared he had, and she ducked away.

"It's not okay," he said, defeat clear in the low dip of his voice.

She gripped his hand, pushing up something she hoped was close to a real smile. "It is." She squeezed his fingers. "We're friends, Matt. That won't change."

Chapter Nineteen
(in which Lauren flies back home for Christmas)

Five more miles and he'd drop her off. Matt would see her onto a plane and hope that the glimpse of her back wouldn't be his last view of her.

We're friends. That won't change.

She'd meant it as a hopeful promise. He'd never felt so devastated.

He wanted, more than anything, for that to change. Not to go away, but to be so much more. The surety of this wish had grown from a tentative inclination when he'd considered the possibility of more while they'd visited his family, to a solid direction of his heart. But the execution of this longing? It proved difficult, complicated by his own stupidity. If only he hadn't turned into a bumbling idiot in front of Katrine. How could he expect Lauren to let that go? He'd acted as though Lauren hadn't meant anything.

She'd said it was fine. He knew it absolutely wasn't, and nothing he'd attempted thus far had proved to her how much he wished back that faulty moment.

Now she was leaving. Yes, with a promise that she'd return. *It's only for Christmas.* He had no reason to doubt her sincerity on that. But what happened when she reconciled with her sister—as he hoped she would so that she'd know peace in that relationship? Would she lose all the reasons she'd had for living on the opposite side of the country from her family? If so, then what?

He'd go find her.

"You can drop me off at the curb." Lauren pointed toward the passenger drop-off zone designated for the airline with whom she traveled.

"Huh?" Snatched from his thoughts, he glanced at Lauren in the passenger's seat.

"Here," she said. "I can check in at the curbside desk and go in."

Not what he'd played out in his mind when he'd offered her a ride to the airport. "I could go in with you."

"You can't go past security. It would be a waste of parking money."

"Not a waste—" he countered.

"A total waste, Matt. Just drop me off."

With nothing to argue, he slowed to a stop at the edge of the curb.

"Thanks." She unsnapped the buckle and opened the door.

Moving quickly, Matt shifted into Park, hopped out of the car, and jogged around to the sidewalk. As she tugged her roll-along luggage from the backseat, he reached around her to get it instead, placing a hand to her lower back. They straightened at the same time, each facing the other.

"Thanks," she said again, this time a little breathy.

He turned the handle of her bag to her. "Is this all?"

"Yes."

Of course it was—it'd been all he'd loaded into the vehicle that morning. Standing less than an arm's length from her, his hands felt empty, the distance between them like too much chilled space. He leaned, cautiously wrapping her in a hug. Though she held stiff, her hands pressed into his back.

"You are returning?" he said.

"I already told you I was."

"Good."

Her head tucked into his shoulder and pressed, and for a moment he thought to lose his fingers in the dark mass of curls he knew to be soft. But then she stepped back, taking with her the clean scent of mint and lavender.

"I'd better get checked in." She spoke to his chest. "You'll tell your family hi for me?"

"Of course."

Tipping her chin upward, she smiled. "Merry Christmas, Matt Murphy."

"Matthew Murphy."

Sassy laughter touched her eyes, making him want to chuckle and to try those lips at the same time. He only allowed one of the two.

"Merry Christmas to you too, Pixie Pants."

She pulled her teeth across her bottom lip, drawing his gaze, testing his self-control, and then she raised on her toes to brush a kiss at his cheek. "Bye, Matt."

Before he could decide to give in to impulse, she was walking away, dragging her luggage. Not looking back.

**

Jackson packed Brayden's Christmas presents into a trash bag and hung them from a tree in the backyard.

Lauren read the text and shook with silent laughter. In the three days since Matt had dropped her off at the airport, they'd kept a running conversation via text—started by him before she'd even boarded the eastbound plane, with *Text me when you land.*

She'd typed *K*, and then they'd carried on a written conversation about not much of anything important until she'd boarded the plane and had to shut her phone off. Several hours later, she'd sent a *Safe on the ground* message, and they'd continued from there.

Getting back to normal, she thought. And there was comfort in it, even if she wished that the last-second parting peck on the cheek had been something more like the kiss they'd shared in the valley. Even if she couldn't let that particular memory fade into the recesses of things gone by and let go. Even if the tenderest parts of her heart didn't want to go back to normal.

Sorry I missed that, she sent back to him. *You took pictures, right?*

I got a video of Brayden climbing the tree to rescue his presents. Sending it to you.

She waited, eyes glued to the screen, eager to witness what was sure to be a scene filled with antics and laughter as only could happen between the Murphy boys. When it blipped as a still image on her phone, she shifted in her soft overstuffed chair and tapped the triangle Play button.

Sure enough, the Murphy boys were at it—laughing and shouting as fourteen-year-old Brayden, clad in green-and-red flannel jammy pants and a Sugar Pine High basketball sweatshirt, climbed through the pine boughs to retrieve his loot. As Lauren chuckled through the ordeal, Ashley padded on fuzzy-socked feet from the hallway to the informal family room, where Lauren had cozied in after their family Christmas dinner.

"What's this?" Ashley lowered to the arm of the chair where Lauren sat.

"A friend's video. His brother is trying to retrieve his presents from a tree in their backyard."

"What?" Ashley responded with an astounded laugh.

"Yeah. They're quite a group. Seven brothers."

"Seven! I can't even imagine."

"It's something. There's always noise—usually laughter. Always something going on."

"Is this the family you spent Thanksgiving with?"

"Yes." Lauren continued watching the video, heart pounding when Brayden lunged for the trash bag, nearly falling out of the cradle of the branches. Helen's yelp in the background proceeded Jackson's laughing declaration that he'd get it.

Ashley leaned in, and Lauren tipped the phone to share the view. Jackson sauntered into the scene carrying a long pole with a basket attached to one end.

"Is that an apple picker?" Ashley asked.

"Looks like it."

Shouts of laughter burst into the video as Jackson easily freed the captive bag while standing safely on the ground. Both girls watching the footage giggled.

"So is that him?" Ashley tapped the screen.

Caught off guard, Lauren jerked her attention to her sister. "Him?"

"The guy who has been texting you all week." Ashley winked. "The one who makes you sparkle."

Heat brushed her face, and Lauren lowered her phone. "I do not sparkle."

Ashley's head tipped back as she laughed. "You're glowing, Lauren. Do you know you literally grin at your phone every time you get a text?"

"No I don't."

"You most certainly do." Ashley reached across Lauren, snatching the phone. "Let's see him again."

"You can't," Lauren argued, too quickly. Then she straightened, cleared her throat. "That's not Matt anyway. It's Jackson, his prankster brother."

"Matt, is it?" A sly grin slipped onto the corners of Ashley's mouth. "Now we're getting somewhere. Does this one of many brothers called Matt have a last name?"

Lauren rolled her eyes. "No. He just goes by Matt, one of seven brothers."

With an unladylike snort, Ashley slid onto the seat of the oversized chair, squishing against Lauren. "Is he a good man?"

Something settled on Lauren. She looked across the room, the lights of the professionally decorated Christmas tree blurring in her vison as she let her mind land on Matt. "Yes," she whispered. "He's a good man."

"He makes you happy."

Lauren didn't have words to answer that. How could happy and ache coexist like this? "It's not what you're thinking, Ash."

Ashley hooked her arm through Lauren's and pulled her in. "Ah. It's complicated?"

Not overly so, but Lauren didn't want to get into it.

"Maybe you're just happy being away from here? From us?"

Though she wanted to ignore the thread of hurt in Ashley's

voice, Lauren couldn't. "That's not true."

Ashley sat up, held a long look on her. "Maybe it's time we're honest, Lauren." She drew in a deep breath. "I'll start. I was mad at you for leaving. It felt like...I don't know, like a slap in the face. I didn't see it coming, and it took a while for me to understand. I thought that..."

The pause suspended between them, and Lauren fought the urge to get up and walk away. She'd had enough difficult conversations lately. And confrontations with Ashley always ended with Lauren's resentful compliance.

Ashley exhaled a shuddered breath. "I thought you were acting out of jealousy."

At that, anger burned. "I have *never* been jealous of you, Ashley. For every one of your lofty accomplishments, I've been proud of you. So very proud. But your life isn't mine. I tried to tell you that when I left. I need my own life, beyond yours and Daddy's shadow."

Though she flinched, Ashley continued to hold her gaze, expression soft—which surprised Lauren. Every other time this kind of conversation dared to rise between them, Ashley would brush Lauren's desires aside, claiming that family duty always came first. Lauren wasn't opposed to family or duty, but at some point, should she stand?

"I see now, sis," Ashley said calmly. "It's taken all these weeks of you being away, but now I see you, and I understand. Politics is in me—my passion. This is how I serve—our family, our neighbors, and our people—and I consider it a privilege. But it isn't you, is it?"

Lauren blinked, partly in disbelief and partly at the relief of finally being heard, finally understood.

"I think," Ashley continued, "that Daddy and I both thought that your means of service was in your administrative skills—and that to our political callings. Perhaps like it was a family calling. It simply made sense to us. But obviously not to you, and that isn't wrong." In a move of uncharacteristic tenderness and humility, Ashley slipped her hands beneath Lauren's and held them. "You are gifted with organization and administration, Lauren. But you should choose how to use those gifts. I see that now, and I'm sorry I didn't get it before."

Finally! Understood, acknowledged. Now Lauren sniffed as she squeezed the hands that held hers. "Thank you, Ashley."

The sisters leaned simultaneously, foreheads touching.

"You are first my sister, Lauren," Ashley said. "Always my sister. And I'm proud of you."

Ah! And this too? So often Lauren had felt less than Ashley, as she felt sure she'd never reach Ashley's high standards and achievements. Now her sister claimed pride in *her*. Such was more than Lauren had dared hoped. With a breathless chuckle, born more of relief than humor, Lauren wrapped her arms around Ashley's shoulders. "I'm proud of you too, sis. You do know that, right?"

"I do." The words quivered on Ashley's voice as she returned the hug. They held there for several breaths, a long-overdue embrace, and finally true understanding.

The beauty of reconciliation. *Now to Him Who is able to do more than you ask or imagine... Amen, and thank You!* Wonder washed in the thought.

Ashley cleared her throat, breathed a wobbly chuckle, and drew back. "You are happy way over on the other side of the country, aren't you?"

"I am." A soft smile curved on Lauren's mouth.

"And this Matt of many brothers..." Ashley left the question hanging.

"He is—" What? So much. So many things.

"Oh dear." Wariness entered Ashley's expression. "That looks like trouble. He's not messing with my kind, talented older sister, is he?"

"No." Lauren looked to her hands, now enfolded again in Ashley's. "No. Like I told you before, he's a good man. Which is proving to be a problem, since we have a pact of friendship, and I own, apparently, a rebellious heart."

"Oh, Lauren." Ashley lifted a hand, ran her fingers over the locks of brown framing Lauren's face, and tucked it behind her ear. "You love him?"

Lauren could only shut her eyes. She would not answer that.

After several beats of silence, during which Lauren remained shuttered behind her lids, trying not to see the handsome face of one she should only regard as a friend, the warmth of Ashley's arms wrapped around her shoulders again.

"I will pray for you," Ashley said.

Five sweet words, which, because Lauren knew Ashley's promise was not simply a platitude, meant so much more than any advice her sister could offer—though Ashley had much more experience in the department of romance. Lauren tucked the sweet promise safe in her heart.

***

He'd let his guard down. Had to be why.

Matt sat with steel in his spine, the spot in his chest that had gone cold at the sight of her now growing hard.

Katrine smiled. Waved. Sauntered toward him and Jackson as they sat in the corner booth at Storm Café. He hadn't thought of her once during this holiday visit. Hadn't wondered if she'd made the despised trip back to this *provincial* mountain town for Christmas. Hadn't even wondered if she'd contacted John.

Didn't care.

Right?

"Dude, are you listening?" Jackson leaned forward.

"What? No." Matt caught up to his response a moment after he'd voiced it. Shaking his head, he shifted his eyes back to his brother. "I mean, yes. Sort of. What were you saying?"

Jackson picked at his unfinished pecan pie and slouched back in his seat. "Forget it."

"No, seriously. I'm sorry. Tell me again."

"I said it's well past old."

"The Jacob-and-Kate thing?"

"No, the milk in the refrigerator." Jackson had a master's

degree in sarcasm.

Matt sighed. He should have been listening to his brother. Honestly, it was a challenge to take him seriously. Rarely did Jackson open up to anyone—let them past his comedic layer and into the deeper places within, where might lurk some issues. Might? No, those issues did lurk, and Matt knew it. Jackson didn't go through life with a significant scar on his upper lip after several surgeries without some bitter blows from jerks who didn't get it—sometimes, shamefully, those jerks being Matt himself, along with the other brothers. Also, there was the Jacob-and-Kate thing, and yeah, it was getting old. For all of them.

Working to focus on his brother, Matt leaned, elbows to table, forward. "Okay, I'm really listening now. Yes, the Jacob-and-Kate thing. It's old. And seriously, buddy, the whole deal was—"

"No." Jackson stared deadpan at him. "See, you weren't listening. At all. I don't want sympathy. Not yours, not Mom's, not Dad's."

Matt's brow pulled in tight. "I...I'm not sure where this is coming from."

Though Jackson continued to stare, the aggravation on his face eased. But the moment the ridged form of his shoulders loosened was the moment Katrine decided to finish her approach.

"Hey there, Murphy boys." Her willowy frame slipped onto the bench beside Jackson. "How's my favorite Sugar Pine men?"

Jackson shifted his glare toward the overly confident woman beside him. "Don't know. Haven't heard from John since you left him at the altar."

Wow. For a man who loved to laugh and make others laugh, Jackson was really in a mood.

Katrine blinked, as if that shot stung. Looked convincing. "That was harsh."

For a moment it seemed this unusual darker version of Jackson was going to hang around—which would have been convenient, as it seemed he'd found a willingness to take up Matt's cause. But then his smile reemerged. Slightly false, but not enough for the likes of Katrine to notice.

"You're right. You know that was just bitterness talking. All the guys in Sugar Pine are thankful knowing we might still have a shot."

Hmm. Still not the comedian. But Katrine either didn't catch Jackson's undercurrent of sarcasm or chose to ignore it. If forced, Matt would have bet on the first.

The injury cleared from her expression, replaced by a brilliant smile. "Oh, Jackson. You always know how to make a girl feel better." Her big brown eyes turned to Matt, all puppy-ish. "Too bad Matt never picked up that skill."

The corners of his eyes tightened. "I recall spending countless hours seeing to your emotional health, Katrine. Perhaps that went unnoticed?"

The sheen in her eyes magically reappeared. "Matthew," she breathed, all hurt and shock.

He pressed his lips together, returning her long look with his own.

Jackson sat up, bounced his gaze from one unmovable face to the other, and then cleared his throat. "Welp. As much fun as the two of you are, I feel I've had enough laughs for the day."

"You're leaving?" Katrine turned a pout toward Jackson.

"Oh yeah." Jackson gathered his coat, picked up his to-go mug, and stood.

Matt mirrored his brother's actions.

"You too?" Katrine whined.

"Jackson's my ride, so..."

"Matthew." There it was. That firm, unarguable voice, somehow infused with some kind of irresistible charm that refused to be put off.

Oh, but he would absolutely refuse this time. Pushing arms into sleeves, he took three steps toward the exit, tossing a folded bill on the table for a tip. And that was as far as he got before her hand latched on to the crook of his elbow, her presence demanding he face her.

Which he did.

"We should talk." She nearly purred.

He stared, mind splitting. *Run*, one half commanded. *Deal with this*, the other countered.

"Please, Matt." Was that sincerity? Did he really glimpse a genuine, unselfish desire in her eyes?

"I can't now," he muttered.

"Okay." Her hand slipped away. "But I really think we should. Things are...complicated now. It'd be best to clear the air, don't you think?"

What would Lauren say? Matt inhaled, wishing with everything in him he hadn't landed himself in the middle of this web of misery.

Of his own making.

"I'll think about it," he said.

She ducked, as if his lack of compliance actually hurt. Then nodded. "Please do."

With that she turned and walked away.

***

Are you sleeping? I hope not. Two things. Dad needs help on a project off grid. Also, ran into Katrine today. She wants to meet. I don't know what to do.

Lauren squeezed her eyes shut, wishing away the burned-in words of Matt's last text. Head pressed against the pile of pillows, she gripped the bulk of her winter comforter and turned her angst to prayer.

Help me want Your best for him.

No matter what that was. But could it possibly be a woman who had spent the last half decade tormenting his heart? Surely not.

I am not God.

Perhaps Katrine had experienced a revelation. What could be better for Matt than to have the desire of his heart finally met?

Give me strength to be unselfish.

Setting aside *Sense and Sensibility*, Lauren drew in a long breath and then opened her eyes.

Perhaps you should meet with her. She might be right. You two might need to talk.

She stared at the words she'd just pecked onto the screen. To delete or to send?

A tap of the screen and it was done. The place of peace that had unfolded with her earlier conversation with Ashley dissolved.

In its place, a storm.

Chapter Twenty
(in which Matt picks Lauren up from the airport)

"What about Lauren?" Mom asked pointedly.

"I texted her earlier." Matt resisted the impulse to push his fingers through his hair. He'd barely slept after Lauren's last text, his mind too busy dissecting her every word—few though they had been—trying to understand the subtext. He'd asked for her honest advice—truthfully hoping she'd tell him to avoid the temptress. Wistfully hoping she'd ask him not to go because...

Yeah. Clearly she wasn't going to do that. Frustrated with all of it, Matt returned to the not-so-comfortable conversation that was unfolding with his parents. "She said she was having a nice time. Would you like me to tell her hi from you?"

Eyebrows lifted, Mom folded her arms. "That is not what I meant, young man."

Matt wanted to growl. "Mom, Lauren and I aren't dating. I made that clear when I brought her here for Thanksgiving."

"Yes. I remember that." Mom's chin tilted up, a gesture she'd gained long ago when her boys grew taller than her average stature and she'd not been willing to let that diminish her authority. "I also remember hoping and praying you'd have enough wherewithal to remedy that situation. Please tell me my faith in your good sense is not misplaced."

Her sharp look and unsheathed intent pierced him through.

Well, Mom, he thought. *I did kiss her. And she kissed me back. Right before she fled from my arms, making everything that seemed perfect between us awkward, because she's sure I don't know what I want and has no intention of being my rebound.*

The silent monologue made that fresh wound throb. Trying to smother the bleed, he returned to the present issue.

"I'm not going on a date with Katrine. This is just a chance to talk. To clear the air."

Mom's raised her eyebrows, and Dad's pursed lips didn't loan any hint of approval.

"It was never you going out with Katrine on a date, son." Dad's firm tone sounded more like he was addressing his teenage boy, not his grown-up son. Which rankled—specifically because of the recent understanding that Matt had acted like a demanding child where the issue of Katrine had been. "That had always been half the concern."

"Now it's *all* the concern," Mom inserted. "You've just stepped out of the snare, Matt. Do you really want to become entangled again?"

"It's not a concern." Matt stepped forward, reminding himself that he was, in fact, that grown-up man, and also, he had, in fact, left behind that not-so-grown-up infatuation with Katrine. On that, he drew a calming breath. Acting like a stubborn teenager wasn't going to prove his case. "I promise," he said more calmly. "I understand now what you guys were worried about. And you were right. She's not good for me—and very likely, I wasn't good for her with all my passive enabling. This is just a conversation so that I don't have to dread coming back to Sugar Pine every time I want to visit, worried that she's going to upend my world all over again. This is me putting an end to that nonsense once and for all."

Surprise bounced on Mom's face, and she looked up at Dad, who's jaw worked back and forth. Finally Dad nodded, looked back at Matt as though he saw him as a man once again.

"That does return us to your mom's first question, Matt." He stepped closer. "What about Lauren?"

Matt shut his eyes, savored the one-hundredth replay, at least, of their kiss at the small tree farm. Hoped that someday—*soon!*—she'd be able to see past his foolishness over Katrine and allow for the chance that he might love her.

Might? No. There was no question there.

"I told her about running into Katrine—asked her what she thought I should do." Matt lifted his head with an openness toward his parents. "She advised this—that I clear things up."

Though confusion folded Mom's brow, she nodded. "Is she...do you..."

He wasn't sure of the ending to either of those unfinished questions, but Matt was fairly certain he didn't have a solid answer for them. Scratch that. He didn't have an answer to one.

"I like her, Mom. More than you do." He winked, hoping to alleviate the strain in the air.

"Ah." That easy smile—slightly mischievous, the likes of which giving undeniable evidence as to where Jackson got his personality—smoothed her features. "How about that, Kevin? Our son does, after all, have good sense."

"Praise God." Kevin laughed, clapping Matt on the shoulder as he passed. "Hopefully, he will pair that with the muscle I need from him up at Falcon's Point in the next few days. It'll be like old times."

Shaking his head, disguising a grin that threatened, Matt skulked toward the stairway. "Glad to know where I stand."

"It *is* good to know such things," Mom said.

"Indeed. Good night," Matt deadpanned.

Their duet of laughter sent him off. Good thing he knew they loved him. That fledgling grin grew full.

Yeah. They loved him well—even when he'd been a blind fool. And he was thankful for it.

***

She felt sick again. This time not because of the flight or the landing.

What she would give to have not made this arrangement before the holidays. The thought of seeing Matt again, there where they'd first met, had become something of torture. She'd missed him way too much. Had relived that kiss Matt hadn't meant, had apologized for, so many times over the past week that she'd lost count. And the past few nights? Agony.

Why had he stopped texting her?

Without looking at the phone, his last text, received three days before, came easily to the surface of her memory.

Meeting Katrine, then going to work with Dad.

That was it. All she knew—all he was going to share. Facing him now, after that long period of silence during which she'd imagined all sorts of not-very-pleasant-to-her-heart events, seemed like a mean joke.

Maybe he wouldn't show up to get her. That would be preferable, because she had no idea how to act. This was a replay of the long, awkward week after Thanksgiving, only worse by tenfold. Now, she not only had the strongly steeped memory of his mouth moving against hers, the mingling of breath and life between them, but she also had this in knowledge that for her, *friends* had shifted. Was no longer enough.

Though he had apologized for that kiss, she could not accept it. Her heart simply—stubbornly—refused.

She was in love with Matthew Murphy. Not just a faint inkling of feelings that could grow. No, that had hit the rearview mirror of her heart sometime between their pretend-to-be-together-because-what-could-be-the-harm escapade gone way too real and Christmas, and she hadn't even known to look as it faded into the backfield. This was hard, all-in, heart-and-mind-gone in love with a man who had told her plainly he had drawn a line between them at friendship and was sorry for that kiss.

Too soon it was time to deboard the plane. The walk through the Jetway became a nerve-racking progression toward hope certain to be cut down. Dropped into the hollow place of wrong man, wrong time. A place of weeping and long-drawn out recovery.

What if, though...

Stepping into the terminal, Lauren dared to dream. What if Matt met her with more than a friendly hug? What if he'd missed her the way she'd missed him and they had a storybook reunion of a pair who only just realized they were in love? Cue the roses. The heart confetti. She nearly sighed as the scene bloomed through her mind. How lovely that would be.

A blast of chilled January air swept over her face as the glass doors parted in front of her. With the whirring sound of her wheeled luggage following close at her heels, Lauren squinted into the brilliant afternoon sun, searching for a red Ford Escape. Didn't take long.

There he was, posed in a sexy slouch, leaning against the hood of his car, hands anchored in his pockets, a confident smirk on that whisker-shadowed face.

A streak of irritation blindsided her as he rose up, casual as you please, eyes pinned on her as if he could read her every secret thought. How dare he show up there, looking that good, gazing at her like that? Who did Matthew Murphy think he was, anyway?

Not her kryptonite. That was for sure. Well, perhaps that wasn't true, but she definitely wasn't going to let him know that.

"Hey there, stranger." He closed the gap of sidewalk between them, voice low, eyes still pinned on her. In a hand he stretched her direction, he held a small bag. "I came prepared."

She looked at what he gripped. A puke bag. Nice. So much for roses. For heart confetti and sappy love-story endings. Nope. To Matt Murphy, she was the woman who threw up on him in the airport.

Looking back at his face, she found that charming-boy smile. "Hi." She refused to smile as she snatched the bag from him. "Thanks." Then she stepped around him, carry-on obediently trailing her.

"Hey." Matt pivoted and then jogged three steps to catch up to her. "You okay?"

"Spiffy."

"Spiffy? Who says *spiffy?*"

"I do. Did. I'm spiffy. And not going to puke on you, but thanks for the concern." She stopped at the back passenger door to his car, clicked on the luggage handle lock, and lowered the pull-behind bar.

As she moved to lift her bag, his hand covered hers. "Lauren?"

Dang if that uncertainty in his voice wasn't...effective. Unable to maintain the quills she'd been working hard to raise, she looked at him again. His brow furrowed; the corners of his eyes pinched. Then he gently tugged the hand he'd captured and drew her into a hug. Torn between wrapping her arms around him and drawing stiffly back, Lauren did neither. Just stood in the circle of his embrace.

A tickle rippled over her scalp as she felt the subtle touch of his fingers grazing the ends of her hair.

Oh why? She thought. *Doesn't he understand?*

Clearly not. With a backward step, she pried space between them.

Smile now gone, Matt blinked, held one last long look on her face—one she refused to meet—and then moved to load her luggage into his car. Without a word, he opened her door. She entered and fastened the seat belt. He slipped into the driver's seat and pulled away.

This was the opposite of her dreams. The most uncomfortable, humiliating, make-her-want-to-sob reverse from what she'd stupidly longed for.

"How was Christmas?" he asked lamely.

"Good."

"That's good."

Her throat tightened. "Yours?" she squawked.

"Good. Funny. Jackson stuck Brayden's—" He cut himself off. "Never mind. You already know that."

"Yes. The video was entertaining. Thank you."

"Of course."

"My sister thought it was funny." Lauren cleared her throat—which felt like it was having an allergic reaction to this pathetic attempt at a conversation. "She thought Jackson was pretty cute."

He glanced at her, then his grip on the steering wheel tightened. "Did she?"

"Yes."

Lauren could feel him continue to tense at her side.

"Anything else?" he said.

She turned toward her window to hide the wrinkle of her face. "Anything else what?"

"Your sister—did she say anything else?"

Weird. "Well, I texted you about the conversation she and I had. That we're better now—actually, things with Ashley and me seem like they're going in a good direction now. But...I already told you that."

"I remember." With that, he seemed to lose interest in furthering this stumbling conversation. Silently, he stared out at the road ahead, driving as if traffic demanded all his concentration.

Muffling a sigh, Lauren sank back into the seat, gripping the grab bar on her door. Though the roads were clear and the sky bright, this trip from the airport to the lodge felt so much longer than the first one had.

It took all her self-discipline not to cry.

Chapter Twenty-One
(in which Matt goes after Lauren)

This had gone on long enough.

Three days too long, actually. Matt had his fill of stiff smiles, stifled conversations, and general discomfort, and it was going to end. That evening.

He'd enlisted Emma's help, which the woman had been glad to give. Actually, she'd eyed him with a tad of condescension, remarking that it'd taken him *too* long and adding that she hadn't understood what under the great big heavens had been holding him back.

Lauren's chill reserve, thank you very much.

What on earth had happened there anyway? One minute she'd been texting him sincere advice about a rather humiliating situation he'd entrusted her with, and then next she was giving him the polite version of the cold shoulder?

Not how he'd envisioned this reunion—not any of it. Leaning against his car three days back, anxious to catch a glimpse of her as she emerged from the airport, he'd had visions of pulling her against him, having her arms encircle his neck, being able to whisper through the soft waves of her hair that he'd missed her more than he could say. Maybe even testing those lips again. His heart had throbbed, head grew light and airy when she'd finally passed through those doors, and he drank in the sight of her—tall brown boots, dark skinny jeans, white sweater under her dark leather jacket. Hair that called to his fingers to feel its soft curls. Deep, beautiful brown eyes. Heart-stopping smile.

All of it dashed the moment that smile had faded into a frown, leaving him swaying in disappointment and bewilderment. Worse, for the past few days, she'd avoided him as much as possible for two people living under the same large roof and working for the same small resort.

All of it ended today. She was going to tell him what had happened—what was so wrong that she couldn't meet his eyes. Why she couldn't summon anything better than a distantly polite *good morning* or *please* or *thank you*.

Now, to find the vexing woman.

He'd checked all the usual places and most of the unexpected. Her apartment. The kitchen. The front desk. All the unoccupied guest rooms. The house. The cabin. The barn. He'd scanned the lakeshore. Checked the trail until it split at the property line. No Lauren. It was as if she was hiding. Avoiding him.

Not as if. She certainly was doing exactly that. But Matt, he had a stubborn streak nestled within his easygoing countenance, and on this, he was not having it. Not today. And if he had any sway over the outcome, not ever again.

"Have you seen Lauren?" He'd circled back to the kitchen, finding Emma and Harold both at the counters. The air hung with a mouthwatering aroma of roasted chicken, rice, steamed vegetables, and baked chocolate. That last of which made him smile despite his agitation as he saw Emma working on the last set of her mini chocolate lava cakes. Lauren's favorite. "Looks amazing, Emma."

"Thanks." She winked. "Made with love and prayers."

He ignored the burn crawling up his neck. "Thanks for that. But have you seen her?"

Harold chuckled. "You two are entertaining."

Awesome. Didn't feel funny, thank you very much.

"She said she was going to head up to the ridge after she finished with the house," Harold mercifully supplied.

"What?"

The older man shrugged. "She's a big girl. Think she'll be fine."

"There's six inches of fresh powder from yesterday's snow." Matt's hands rolled into fists. "She's only snowshoed once before, and the trail's not marked well."

Harold and Emma exchanged a look—one Matt found a tad on the patronizing side. He was *not* overreacting. After an extended draw of silence, Emma spoke up. "Guess you'd better go make sure she finds her way. Not that I doubt she will."

Ugh. Could no one just cooperate with him on this? Wouldn't it be perfect if Lauren would quit running away from things that made her uncomfortable and just deal with it?

Well. They'd never have met, then. And he was one to point fingers, Mr. Ran Out on His Best Friend's Wedding.

Rolling his shoulders, trying to shake the bad mood, Matt turned. "Thanks."

It was a good day to be on a trail. He had to admit that as he strapped on his snowshoes, gripped the poles, and set out down the trail. Blue sky, warm sunshine, only a hint of a breeze. A nice change from yesterday's snowstorm.

Matt shifted his rumpled attitude as he focused his mind on prayer. Lauren would have a verse of praise ready on the tip of her tongue. What was the one she'd said when they'd been on the ridge together? Something about God's handiwork. Man, he needed to work harder at that memorizing thing.

As he scaled the final climb to the flat open spot of the ridge, Lauren came into view. Snuggled in her white coat and hat, she sat beneath the arbor he and his dad had fashioned of cedar several years back. She stared at the lake below.

"Lauren." He continued his pack, pack, pack, step motion through the loose powder, firming the trail Lauren had cut.

The rise and fall of her shoulders betrayed her sigh, and she didn't look at him. "Hey. I wondered if that was you."

"Oh?"

"I could hear you tramping down the snow for the last five

minutes."

"I see." Two more steps and he'd be beside her. "Is that a disappointment?" Did he really want an answer?

She lifted her chin, and a jolt of pain sparked in his chest at the sight of unshed tears. "I guess it's time."

"Time?" He lowered onto the bench next to her.

"To be honest."

Angling toward her, he nodded. "I'd like that."

When he thought she'd finally tell him why she'd been so cold recently, her attention settled back on the lake.

"Talk to me, Lauren."

"I think it's you who should talk to me."

"Okay..." Should he start with how much he missed her? Or ask why she was shutting him out? "I think you're mad at me, but I don't know why."

"You don't?" Pursed lips and furrowed brow turned toward him. "Truly, you don't?"

"I really don't, Lauren, and it's frustrating that you won't tell me."

"Three days, Matt!"

This was the angriest he'd ever seen her, but his own ire was tempered by the sight of her blinking back tears.

"Three days of this silence between us since you came back? Yeah, that's pretty irritating."

"No. Three days of silence from *you*. Over Christmas. I can't play this game anymore—or be this...I don't know. Whatever it is you think I am."

Three days of silence from him when?

Oh.

Oh man. Yikes.

"Lauren, I thought I texted you that I'd be off grid."

"What?"

"When I texted you about Katrine, I told you two things—that she'd found me and that I was going to go work on a project with my dad off grid."

She sniffed. Stared at him, leaving him to wonder if she didn't believe his claim.

"Off grid?" she said.

"Yes. Falcon's Point, where Dad was putting up a new tiny house for a minimalist community, is off grid. You have to travel twenty miles to get a signal."

"I thought off grid meant something about electricity."

"Yes. That. And some communities don't get a cell signal. Like Falcon's Point."

Her expression tightened with skepticism. "And you were there for three days?"

"Two and a half, but yes. Even tiny houses take time." And actually, they'd put that one up in record time, because Matt needed to get back to Lake Shore so he could pick Lauren up from the airport.

Her shoulders rolled in as she slumped forward. "Oh," she breathed.

"Did you really think I was ignoring you?"

The rigid shifting of her jaw concerned him.

"I thought..." She swallowed, glanced at him, but then looked at her hands. "Did you meet with Katrine?"

Ah. Now it all made sense. "Yes. I did—because you told me I should."

She nodded. "How...how did that go?"

Matt drew in a breath. This he hadn't intended to delay so long. He'd needed to tell her about that super-awkward, hopefully-for-the-last-time encounter. But it wasn't what he'd wanted to lead with.

In his hesitation, Lauren stood. "It's not my business, Matt."

"Yes, it is." He rose beside her, catching her hand before she could step away. "I want to tell you."

She shut her eyes. Likely praying. Which was a good idea. *Help me not to mess this up, because this part's sticky.* He touched her shoulder, then turned her to face him. "She didn't want to clear the air—not the way I did. She said she realized what had been in front of her all along, and that her toying had been hurtful, and that she and John were over. Then—" He gulped, looked at his feet, and wished away the color certainly flooding his face. Forcing himself to find her eyes, he gripped her elbow. "She kissed me."

A hard chill fell over her face, and she stepped back, holding her hand up. "You know what, Matt? I'm going back to my original claim. I don't want to—"

He caught her backward retreat, this time hands on both elbows. "Lauren, don't. Just...listen."

"Matt, I can't do this." A sob caught her words.

"Please?" He waited in the frozen silence, half expecting her to walk away. When she didn't, he drew in a new breath. "She kissed an ice sculpture, Lauren. I swear, and as soon as I regathered my blindsided wits, I put enough space between her and me to build a new solar system." Just touching on the memory of Katrine's desperate attempt at...seduction?—he had no idea what to name it, other than pathetic—made him tense with anger. And then he felt conviction—because how could he have spent so long chasing after someone so shallow, so selfish? What exactly did that make him?

Repentant, that's what.

"Lauren." He stepped closer, filling the gap between them as he whispered her name. She didn't back away, and he was thankful. "I have no idea why for so many years I told God that what I wanted was what was best and demanding that He give it to me. Such an arrogant fool. Such a childish way to live, and I'm ashamed of it. But when I see you, Lauren, I'm so thankful God doesn't always give us everything we ask for. So thankful that He is willing to tell us no—tell me no. Because now I see that He knew so much better than I.

"And as for the kiss..." Sliding his hand up her arm, he found her face and cupped it with his palm. When the pad of his thumb brushed her cheekbone, she finally met his gaze. "I wanted it to be you."

Finally, her stiff frame eased, and as a tear leaked from the corner of her eye, he leaned to touch her forehead with his.

"What?" she said with near disbelief.

The breath of her whisper fanned over his lips. An irresistible temptation. Fearing her rejection, he tested her lips with the lightest brush of his.

"Matt..." Her hands found the front of his coat and gripped. "Promise you're not teasing. I can't handle that—not about this."

With the smallest movement, he shook his head. "I wanted it to be you, Lauren." As proof, he tried her mouth again, lengthening the kiss as she leaned against him. His hands slipped into her hair, and on a breath, he pulled away.

"Me?" she asked with wonder.

"Yes, you." He traced the arc of her top lip with the pad of his thumb. Kissed her eyelids. Her nose. The soft, full lip he'd just touched. "I want it to be always you."

As she moved deeper into his embrace, a confession of love on her teary voice—the best thing he'd heard in his life—it occurred to him afresh how much better God's plans were than his own. And he was thankful for the nos that had led him to this. To Lauren—the woman who had puked on him at the airport.

A woman who made him want to be so much more.

The End

(in which we know is only the beginning)

Dear reader

I hope you enjoyed Matt and Lauren's story and that it encouraged you in your own personal walk with the Lord. I'd so appreciate it if you'd leave your thoughts on the story in the form of a review on Amazon or Goodreads (or both!). You'll find further inspiration and encouragement on The Potter's House Books

Website (www.pottershousebooks.com) and by reading the other books in the series. Read them all and be encouraged and uplifted!

Find all the books on Amazon and on The Potter's House Books website:

Book 1: *The Hope We Share*, by Juliette Duncan
Book 2: *Beyond the Deep*, by Kristen M. Fraser
Book 3: *Honor's Reward*, by Mary Manners
Book 4: *Hands of Grace*, by Brenda S. Anderson
Book 5: *Always You*, by Jen Rodewald
Book 6: *Her Cowboy Forever*, by Dora Hiers
Book 7: *Changed Somehow*, by Chloe Flanagan
Books 8: *Fragrance of Forgiveness*, by Delia Latham
Books 9-24 to be announced

Questions for thought:

1. In *Always You*, Lauren has left home looking for a chance at a life of independence. Have you ever left a situation looking for a new start? Did you feel like you were running away, or were you stepping out in faith?

2. When Matt declares that he's a Christian, Lauren challenges him with a question about his favorite verse. Do you feel knowing Scripture is an important part of the Christian life?

3. Matt is wrestling with frustration at life—more specifically with God because of the way something did not work out in his life. Have you ever felt betrayed or let down by God? What did you do with that sense of frustration?

4. Matt is part of a large family—the oldest of seven brothers! What are your family dynamics, and do you feel like that shaped who you are now?

5. Lauren has a tricky relationship with her sister—sometimes she struggles with a sense of inferiority and sometimes with a feeling of being used and then overlooked. Relationships can be tricky like that. Have you ever struggled with a loved one, and if you're willing to share, were you able to overcome some of those issues?

6. Matt's practice of daily Bible reading is something that draws Lauren's admiration. In the story, we find out he's imitating his dad. How important is it for parents to model their walk with Jesus? In what other ways can this modeling be done?

7. A major theme of *Always You* is trusting the Master Potter's plan—especially when His answer to our desire is a solid no. Has God ever told you no? Have you ever had to "trust in the Lord with all your heart, and lean not on your own understanding" in a matter that, honestly, you found disappointing?

Jennifer Rodewald

About the Author

Jennifer Rodewald, a.k.a. J. Rodes, lives on the wide plains somewhere near the middle of Nowhere. A coffee addict and storyteller, she also wears the hats of mom, teacher, and friend. Mostly, she loves Jesus and wants to see others fall in love with Him too.

She would love to hear from you! Please visit her at https://authorjenrodewald.com/ or at www.facebook.com/authorjenrodewald.

Always You

Made in the USA
Middletown, DE
11 November 2021